Frederick The Great And His Family

A Historical Novel
Book IV

by

L. Mühlbach

Frederick The Great And His Family
A Historical Novel
Book IV

by L. Mühlbach

ISBN: 978-93-62201-29-4

Published by

DOUBLE 9 BOOKS

2/13-B, Ansari Road
Daryaganj, New Delhi – 110002
info@double9books.com
www.double9books.com
Tel. 011-40042856

ABOUT THE AUTHOR

Luise Muhlbach, born Clara Maria Regina Muller on January 2, 1814, in Neubrandenburg, Germany, was a renowned German writer acclaimed for her historical fiction. Writing under the pseudonym Luise Muhlbach, she captivated readers with vivid narratives that brought history to life. Despite a relatively short-lived period of popularity, her works continue to resonate with audiences. Born to Friedrich Andreas Müller and Friederika Müller (nee Strübing), Clara displayed early literary talent that flourished into a prolific career. Her most famous novel, "Frederick the Great and His Court" (German: Friedrich der Grosse und sein Hof), stands as a testament to her narrative prowess. This and many other works were translated into English, broadening her reach and influence. Muhlbach's storytelling skill lay in her ability to intertwine historical accuracy with compelling characters and plotlines, transporting readers to different epochs with ease. Through her writing, she illuminated the complexities of bygone eras, offering insights into the lives of prominent figures and the societies they inhabited. Though she passed away on September 26, 1873, in Berlin, Muhlbach's literary legacy endures, ensuring that her contributions to the genre of historical fiction remain cherished and celebrated by generations of readers worldwide.

CONTENTS

CHAPTER I
THE KING AND HIS OLD AND NEW ENEMIES

Three years, three long, terrible years had passed since the beginning of this fearful war; since King Frederick of Prussia had stood alone, without any ally but distant England, opposed by all Europe.

These three years had somewhat undeceived the proud and self-confident enemies of Frederick. The pope still called him the Marquis of Brandenburg, and the German emperor declared that, notwithstanding the adverse circumstances threatening him on every side, the King of Prussia was still a brave and undaunted adversary. His enemies, alter having for a long time declared that they would extinguish him and reduce him once more to the rank of the little Prince-Elector of Brandenburg, now began to fear him. From every battle, from every effort, from every defeat, King Frederick rose up with a clear brow and flashing eye, and unshaken courage. Even the lost battles did not cast a shadow upon the lustre of his victories. In both the one and the other he had shown himself a hero, greater even after the battles in his composure and decision, in his unconquerable energy, in the circumspection and presence of mind by which he grasped at a glance all the surroundings, and converted the most threatening into favorable circumstances. After a great victory his enemies might indeed say they had conquered the King of Prussia, but never that they had subdued him. He stood ever undaunted, ever ready for the contest, prepared to attack them when they least expected it; to take advantage of every weak point, and to profit by every incautious movement. The fallen ranks of his brave soldiers appeared to be dragons' teeth, which produced armed warriors.

In the camps of the allied Austrians, Saxons, and Russians hunger and sickness prevailed. In Vienna, Petersburg, and Dresden, the costs and burden of the war were felt to be almost insupportable. The Prussian army was healthy, their magazines well stocked, and, thanks to the English subsidy, the treasury seemed inexhaustible. Three years, as we have said, of never-ceasing struggle had gone by. The heroic brow of the great Frederick had been wreathed with new laurels. The battles of Losovitz, of Rossbach, of Leuthen, and of Zorndorf were such dazzling victories that they were not even obscured by the defeats of Collin and Hochkirch. The allies made their shouts of victory resound throughout all Europe, and used every means to produce the impression upon the armies and the people that these victories were decisive.

Another fearful enemy, armed with words of Holy Writ, was now added to the list of those who had attacked him with the sword. This new adversary was Pope Clement XIII. He mounted the apostolic throne in May, 1758, and immediately declared himself the irreconcilable foe of the little Marquis of Brandenburg, who had dared to hold up throughout Prussia all superstition and bigotry to mockery and derision; who had illuminated the holy gloom and obscurity of the church with the clear light of reason and truth; who misused the priests and religious orders, and welcomed and assisted in Prussia all those whom the holy mother Catholic Church banished for heresies and unbelief.

Benedict, the predecessor of the present pope, was also known to have been the enemy of Frederick, but he was wise enough to be silent and not draw down upon the cloisters, and colleges, and Catholics of Prussia the rage of the king.

But Clement, in his fanatical zeal, was not satisfied to pursue this course. He was resolved to do battle against this heretical king. He fulminated the anathemas of the church and bitter imprecations against him, and showered down words of blessing and salvation upon all those who declared themselves his foes. Because of this fanatical hatred, Austria received a new honor, a new title from the hands of the pope. As a reward for her enmity to this atheistical marquis, and the great service which she had rendered in this war, the pope bestowed the title of apostolic majesty upon the empress and her successors. Not only the royal house of Austria, but the generals and the whole army of pious and believing Christians, should know and feel that the blessing of the pope rested upon their arms, protecting them from adversity and defeat. The glorious victory of Hochkirch must be solemnly celebrated, and the armies of the allies incited to more daring deeds of arms.

For this reason, Pope Clement sent to Field-Marshal Daun, who had commanded at the battle of Hochkirch, a consecrated hat and sword, thus changing this political into a religious war. It was no longer a question of earthly possessions, but a holy contest against an heretical enemy of mother church. Up to this time, these consecrated gifts had been only bestowed upon generals who had already subdued unbelievers or subjugated barbarians. *[Footnote: OEuvres Posthumes, vol. iii.]*

But King Frederick of Prussia laughed at these attacks of God's vicegerent. To his enemies, armed with the sword, he opposed his own glittering blade; to his popish enemy, armed with the tongue and the pen, he opposed the same weapons. He met the first in the open field, the last in winter quarters, through those biting, mocking, keen Fliegenden Blattern, which at that time made all Europe roar with laughter, and crushed and brought to nothing the great deeds of the pope by the curse of ridicule.

The consecrated hat and sword of Field-Marshal Daun lost its value through the letter of thanks from Daun to the pope, which the king intercepted, and which, even in Austria, was laughed at and made sport of.

The congratulatory letter of the Princess Soubise to Daun was also made public, and produced general merriment.

When the pope called Frederick the "heretical Marchese di Brandenburgo," the king returned the compliment by calling him the "Grand Lama," and delighted himself over the assumed infallibility of the vicegerent of the Most High.

But the king not only scourged the pope with his satirical pen—the modest and prudish Empress Maria Theresa was also the victim of his wit. He wrote a letter, supposed to be from the Marquise de Pompadour to the Queen of Hungary, in which the inexplicable friendship between the virtuous empress and the luxurious mistress of Louis was mischievously portrayed. This letter of Frederick's was spread abroad in every direction, and people were not only naive enough to read it, but to believe it genuine. The Austrian court saw itself forced to the public declaration that all these letters were false; that Field-Marshal Daun had not received a consecrated wig, but a hat; and that the empress had never received a letter of this character from the Marquise de Pompadour. *[Footnote: In this letter the marquise complained bitterly that the empress had made it impossible for her to hasten to Vienna and offer her the homage, the lore, the friendship she cherished for her in her heart. The empress had established a court of virtue and modesty in Vienna, and this tribunal could hardly receive the Pompadour graciously. The marquise, therefore, entreated the empress to execute judgment against this fearful tribunal of virtue, and to bow to the yoke of the omnipotent goddess Venus. All these letters can be seen in the "Supplement aux OEuvres Posthumes."]* These Fliegende Blattern, as we have said, were the weapons with which King Frederick fought against his enemies when the rough, inclement winter made it impossible for him to meet them in the open field. In the winter quarters in 1758 most of those letters appeared; and no one but the Marquis d'Argens, the most faithful friend of Frederick, guessed who was the author of these hated and feared satires.

The enemies of the king also made use of this winter rest to make every possible aggression; they had their acquaintances and spies throughout

Germany; under various pretenses and disguises, they were scattered abroad—even in the highest court circles of Berlin they were zealously at work. By flattery, and bribery, and glittering promises, they made friends and adherents, and in the capital of Prussia they found ready supporters and informers. They were not satisfied with this—they were haughty and bold enough to seek for allies among the Prussians, and hoped to obtain entrance into the walls of the cities, and possession of the fortresses by treachery.

The Austrian and Russian prisoners confined in the fortress of Kustrin conspired to give it up to the enemy. The number of Russian prisoners sent to the fortress of Kustrin after the battle of Zorndorf, was twice as numerous as the garrison, and if they could succeed in getting possession of the hundred cannon captured at Zorndorf, and placed as victorious trophies in the market-place, it would be an easy thing to fall upon and overcome the garrison.

This plan was all arranged, and about to be carried out, but it was discovered the day before its completion. The Prussian commander doubled the guard before the casemates in which three thousand Russian prisoners were confined, and arrested the Russian officers. Their leader, Lieutenant von Yaden of Courland, was accused, condemned by the court-martial, and, by the express command of the king, broken upon the wheel. Even this terrible example bore little fruit. Ever new attempts were being made—ever new conspiracies discovered amongst the prisoners; and whilst the armies of the allies were attacking Prussia outwardly, the prisoners were carrying on a not less dangerous guerilla war—the more to be feared because it was secret—not in the open field and by day, but under the shadow of night and the veil of conspiracy.

Nowhere was this warfare carried on more vigorously than in Berlin. All the French taken at Rossbach, all the Austrians captured at Leuthen, and the Russian officers of high rank taken at Zorndorf, had been sent by the king to Berlin. They had the most enlarged liberty; the whole city was their prison, and only their word of honor bound them not to leave the walls of Berlin. Besides this, all were zealous to alleviate the sorrows of the "poor captives," and by fetes and genial amusements to make them forget their captivity. The doors of all the first houses were opened to the distinguished strangers—everywhere they were welcome guests, and there was no assembly at the palace to which they were not invited.

Even in these fearful times, balls and fetes were given at the court. Anxious and sad faces were hidden under gay masks, and the loud sound of music and dancing drowned the heavy sighs of the desponding. While the Austrians, Russians, and Prussians strove with each other on the bloody battle-field, the Berlin ladies danced the graceful Parisienne dances with the noble prisoners. This was now the mode.

Truly there were many aching hearts in this gay and merry city, but they hid their grief and tears in their quiet, lonely chambers, and their clouded brows cast no shadow upon the laughing, rosy faces of the beautiful women whose brothers, husbands, and lovers, were far away on the bloody battle-field If not exactly willing to accept these strangers as substitutes, they were at least glad to seek distraction in their society. After all, it is impossible to be always mourning, always complaining, always leading a cloistered life. In the beginning, the oath of constancy and remembrance, which all had sworn at parting, had been religiously preserved, and Berlin had the physiognomy of a lovely, interesting, but dejected widow, who knew and wished to know nothing of the joys of life. But suddenly Nature had asserted her own inexorable laws, which teach forgetfulness and inspire hope. The bitterest ears were dried—the heaviest sighs suppressed; people had learned to reconcile themselves to life, and to snatch eagerly at every ray of sunshine which could illumine the cold, hopeless desert, which surrounded them.

They had seen that it was quite possible to live comfortably, even while wild war was blustering and raging without—that weak, frail human nature, refused to be ever strained, ever excited, in the expectation of great events. In the course of these three fearful years, even the saddest had learned again to laugh, jest, and be gay, in spite of death and defeat. They loved their fatherland—they shouted loudly and joyfully over the great victories of their king—they grieved sincerely over his defeats; but they could not carry their animosities so far as to be cold and strange to the captive officers who were compelled by the chances of war to remain in Berlin.

They had so long striven not to seek to revenge themselves upon these powerless captives, that they had at last truly forgotten they were enemies; and these handsome, entertaining, captivating, gallant gentlemen were no longer looked upon even as prisoners, but as strangers and travellers, and therefore they should receive the honors of the city. [Footnote: Sulzer writes: "The prisoners of war are treated here as if they were distinguished travellers and visitors."]

The king commanded that these officers should receive all attention. It was also the imperative will of the king that court balls should be given; he wished to prove to the world that his family were neither sad nor dispirited, but gay, bold, and hopeful.

CHAPTER II
THE THREE OFFICERS

It was the spring of 1759. Winter quarters were broken up, and it was said the king had left Breslau and advanced boldly to meet the enemy. The Berlin journals contained accounts of combats and skirmishes which had taken place here and there between the Prussians and the allies, and in which, it appeared, the Prussians had always been unfortunate.

Three captive officers sat in an elegant room of a house near the castle, and conversed upon the news of the day, and stared at the morning journals which lay before them on the table.

"I beg you," said one of them in French—"I beg you will have the goodness to translate this sentence for me. I think it has relation to Prince Henry, but I find it impossible to decipher this barbarous dialect." He handed the journal to his neighbor, and pointed with his finger to the paragraph.

"Yes, there is something about Prince Henry," said the other, with a peculiar accent which betrayed the Russian; "and something, Monsieur Belleville, which will greatly interest you."

"Oh, I beseech you to read it to us," said the Frenchman, somewhat impatiently; then, turning graciously to the third gentleman who sat silent and indifferent near him, he added: "We must first ascertain, however, if our kind host, Monsieur le Comte di Ranuzi, consents to the reading."

"I gladly take part," said the Italian count, "in any thing that is interesting; above all, in every thing which has no relation to this wearisome and stupid Berlin."

"Vraiment! you are right." sighed the Frenchman. "It is a dreary and ceremonious region. They are so inexpressibly prudish and virtuous—so ruled with old-fashioned scruples—led captive by such little prejudices that I should be greatly amused at it, if I did not suffer daily from the dead monotony it brings. What would the enchanting mistress of France—what would the Marquise de Pompadour say, if she could see me, the gay, witty, merry Belleville, conversing with such an aspect of pious gravity with this poor Queen of Prussia, who makes a face if one alludes to La Pucelle d'Orleans, and wishes to make it appear that she has not read Crebillon!"

"Tell me, now, Giurgenow, how is it with your court of Petersburg? Is it formal, as ceremonious as here in Prussia?"

Giurgenow laughed aloud. "Our Empress Elizabeth is an angel of beauty and goodness—mild and magnanimous to all-sacrificing herself constantly to the good of others. Last year she gave a ball to her body-guard. She danced with every one of the soldiers, and sipped from every glass; and when the soldiers, carried away by her grace and favor, dared to indulge in somewhat free jests, the good empress laughed merrily, and forgave them. On that auspicious day she first turned her attention to the happy Bestuchef. He was then a poor subordinate officer—now he is a prince and one of the richest men in Russia."

"It appears that your Russia has some resemblance to my beautiful France," said Belleville, gayly. "But how is it with you, Count Ranuzi? Is the Austrian court like the court of France, or like this wearisome Prussia?"

"The Austrian court stands alone—resembles no other," said the Italian, proudly. "At the Austrian court we have a tribunal of justice to decide all charges against modesty and virtue The Empress Maria Theresa is its president."

"Diable!" cried the Frenchman, "what earthly chance would the Russian empress and my lovely, enchanting marquise have, if summoned before this tribunal by their most august ally the Empress Maria Theresa? But you forget, Giurgenow, that you have promised to read us something from the journal about Prince Henry."

"It is nothing of importance," said the Russian, apathetically; "the prince has entirely recovered from his wounds, and has been solacing himself in his winter camp at Dresden with the representations upon the French stage. He has taken part as actor, and has played the role of Voltaire's Enfant Prodigue. It is further written, that he has now left the comic stage and commenced the graver game of arms."

"He might accidentally change these roles," said Belleville, gayly, "and play the Enfant Prodigue when he should play the hero. In which would he be the greater, do you know, Ranuzi?"

The Italian shrugged his shoulders. "You must ask his wife."

"Or Baron Kalkreuth, who has lingered here for seven months because of his wounds," said Giurgenow, with a loud laugh. "Besides, Prince Henry is averse to this war, all his sympathies are on our side. If the fate of war should cost the King of Prussia his life, we would soon have peace and leave this detestable Berlin—this dead, sandy desert, where we are now languishing as prisoners."

"The god of war is not always complaisant," said the Frenchman, grimly. "He does not always strike those whom we would gladly see fall; the balls often go wide of the mark."

"Truly a dagger is more reliable," said Ranuzi, coolly.

The Russian cast a quick, lowering side glance upon him.

"Not always sure," said he. "It is said that men armed with daggers have twice found their way into the Prussian camp, and been caught in the king's tent. Their daggers have been as little fatal to the king as the cannon-balls."

"Those who bore the daggers were Dutchmen," said Ranuzi, apathetically; "they do not understand this sort of work. One must learn to handle the dagger in my fatherland."

"Have you learned?" said Giurgenow, sharply.

"I have learned a little of every thing. I am a dilettanti in all."

"But you are master in the art of love," said Belleville, smiling. "Much is said of your love-affairs, monsieur."

"Much is said that is untrue." said the Italian, quietly. "I love no intrigues—least of all, love intrigues; while you, sir, are known as a veritable Don Juan. I learn that you are fatally in love with the beautiful maid of honor of the Princess Henry."

"Ah, you mean the lovely Fraulein von Marshal," said Giurgenow; "I have also heard this, and I admire the taste and envy the good fortune of Belleville."

"It is, indeed, true," said Belleville; "the little one is pretty, and I divert myself by making love to her. It is our duty to teach these little Dutch girls, once for all, what true gallantry is."

"And is that your only reason for paying court to this beautiful girl?" said Giurgenow, frowningly.

"The only reason, I assure you," cried Belleville, rising up, and drawing near the window. "But, look," cried he, hastily; "what a crowd of men are filling the streets, and how the people are crying and gesticulating, as if some great misfortune had fallen upon them!"

The two officers hastened to his side and threw open the window. A great crowd of people was indeed assembled in the platz, and they were still rushing from the neighboring streets into the wide, open square, in the middle of which, upon a few large stones, a curious group were exhibiting themselves.

There stood a tall, thin man enveloped in a sort of black robe; his long gray hair fell in wild locks around his pallid and fanatical countenance. In his right hand he held a Bible, which he waved aloft to the people, while his large, deeply-set, hollow eyes were raised to heaven, and his pale lips murmured light and unintelligible words. By his side stood a woman, also in black, with dishevelled hair floating down her back. Her face was colorless, she looked like a corpse, and her thin, blue lips were pressed together as if in death. There was life in her eyes—a gloomy, wild, fanatical fire flashed from them. Her glance was glaring and uncertain, like a will-o'-the-wisp, and filled those upon whom it fell with a shivering, mysterious feeling of dread.

And now, as if by accident, she looked to the windows where the three gentlemen were standing. The shadow of a smile passed over her face, and she bowed her head almost imperceptibly. No one regarded this; no one saw that Giurgenow answered this greeting, and smiled back significantly upon this enigmatical woman.

"Do you know what this means, gentlemen?" said Belleville.

"It means," said Giurgenow, "that the people will learn from their great prophet something of the continuance, or rather of the conclusion of this war. These good, simple people, as it seems to me, long for rest, and wish to know when they may hope to attain it. That man knows, for he is a great prophet, and all his prophecies are fulfilled."

"But you forget to make mention of the woman?" said Ranuzi, with a peculiar smile.

"The woman is, I think, a fortune-teller with cards, and the Princess Amelia holds her in great respect; but let us listen to what the prophet says."

They were silent, and listened anxiously. And now the voice of the prophet raised itself high above the silent crowd. Pealing and sounding through the air, it fell in trumpet-tones upon the ear, and not one word escaped the eager and attentive people.

"Brothers," cried the prophet, "why do you interrupt me? Why do you disturb me, in my quiet, peaceful path—me and this innocent woman, who stood by my side last night, to read the dark stars, and whose soul is sad, even as my own, at what we have seen."

"What did you see?" cried a voice from the crowd.

"Pale, ghostly shadows, who, in bloody garments, wandered here and there, weeping and wailing, seating themselves upon a thousand open graves, and singing out their plaintive hymns of lamentation. 'War! war!' they cried, 'woe to war! It kills our men, devours our youths, makes widows of our women, and nuns of our maidens. Woe, woe to war! Shriek out a prayer to God for peace—peace! O God, send us peace; close these open graves, heal our wounds, and let our great suffering cease!'"

The prophet folded his hands and looked to heaven, and now the woman's voice was heard.

"But the heavens were dark to the prayer of the spirits, and a blood-red stream gushed from them; colored the stars crimson, turned the moon to a lake of blood, and piteous voices cried out from the clouds, and in the air—'Fight on and die, for your king wills it so; your life belongs to him, your blood is his.' Then, from two rivulets of blood, giant-like, pale, transparent forms emerged; upon the head of the first, I read the number, '1759.' Then the pale form opened its lips, and cried out: 'I bring war, and ever-new bloodshed. Your king demands the blood of your sons; give it to him. He demands your gold; give it to him. The king is lord of your body, your blood, and your soul. When he speaks, you must obey!'"

"It seems to me all this is a little too Russian in its conception," said Ranuzi, half aloud. "I shall be surprised if the police do not interrupt this seance, which smells a little of insurrection."

"The scene is so very piquant," said Giurgenow, "I would like to draw nearer. Pardon me, gentlemen, I must leave you, and go upon the square. It is interesting to hear what the people say, and how they receive such prophecies. We can, perhaps, judge in this way of the probabilities of peace and liberty. The voice of the people is, in politics, ever the decisive voice." He took his hat, and, bowing to the gentlemen, left the room hastily.

CHAPTER III
RANUZI

Count Ranuzi gazed after the Russian with a mocking smile. "Do you know, Belleville, where he is going?"

"He has not told us, but I guess it. He is going to approach this fortune-teller, and give her a sign that her zeal has carried her too far, and that, if not more prudent, she will betray herself."

"You think, then, that Giurgenow knows the fortune-teller?"

"I am certain of it. He has engaged these charlatans to rouse up the people, and excite them against the king. This is, indeed, a very common mode of proceeding, and often successful; but here, in Prussia, it can bear no fruit. The people here have nothing to do with politics; the king reigns alone. The people are nothing but a mass of subjects, who obey implicitly his commands, even when they know, that in so doing, they rush on destruction."

"Giurgenow has failed, and he might have counted upon failure! If you, Belleville, had resorted to these means, I could have understood it. In France, the people play an important role in politics. In order to put down the government, you must work upon the people. You might have been forgiven for this attempt, but Giurgenow never!"

"You believe, then, that he is manoeuvring here, in Berlin, in the interest of his government?" said Belleville, amazed.

Ranuzi laughed heartily. "That is a fine and diplomatic mode of expressing the thing!" said he. "Yes, he is here in the interest of his government; but when the Prussian government becomes acquainted with this fact, they will consider him a spy. If discovered, he will be hung. If successful, when once more at liberty, he may receive thanks and rewards from Russia. See, now, how rightly I have prophesied! There is Giurgenow, standing by the side of the prophetess, and I imagine I almost hear the words he is whispering to her. She will commence again to prophesy, but in a less violent and fanatical manner."

"No, no; she will prophesy no more! The police are breaking their way forcibly through the crowd. They do not regard the cries of fear and suffering of those they are shoving so violently aside. These are the servants of the police; they will speedily put an end to this prophesying. Already the people are flying. Look how adroitly Giurgenow slips away, and does not condescend to give a glance to the poor prophetess he inspired. Only see how little respect these rough policemen have for these heaven-inspired prophets! They seize them rudely, and bear them off. They will be punished with, at least, twenty-four hours' arrest. In Prussia, this concourse and tumult of the people is not allowed. Come, monsieur, let us close the window; the comedy is over. The prophets are in the watch-house. Their role is probably forever played out!" said Belleville, smilingly.

"Not so; they will recommence it to-morrow. These same prophets have high and mighty protectors in Berlin; the police will not dare to keep them long under arrest. The Princess Amelia will demand her fortune-teller."

"Vraiment, monsieur le comte," said the Frenchman, "you seem extraordinarily well acquainted with all these intrigues?"

"I observe closely," said Ranuzi, with a meaning smile. "I am very silent—therefore hear a great deal."

"Well, I counsel you not to give to me or my actions the honor of your observations," said Belleville. "My life offers few opportunities for discovery. I live, I eat, I sleep, I chat, and write poetry and caress, and seek to amuse myself as well as possible. Sometimes I catch myself praying to God tearfully for liberty, and truly, not from any political considerations—simply from the selfish wish to get away from here. You see, therefore, I am an innocent and harmless bon enfant, not in the least troubled about public affairs."

"No," said Ranuzi, "you do not love Fraulein Marshal at all from political reasons, but solely because of her beauty, her grace, and her charms. Behold, this is the result of my observations."

"You have, then, been watching me?" said Belleville, blushing. "I have told you that I was always observant. This is here my only distraction and recreation, and really I do not know what I should do with my time if I did not kill the weary hours in this way."

"You do employ it sometimes to a better purpose?" said the Frenchman, in low tones. "Love is still for you a more agreeable diversion, and you understand the game well."

"It appears you are also an observer," said Ranuzi, with an ironical smile. "Well, then, I do find love a sweeter diversion; and if I should yield myself up entirely to my love-dreams, I would perhaps be less observant. But, Belleville, why do you take your hat? Will you also leave me?"

"I must, perforce. Through our agreeable conversation I had entirely forgotten that I had promised Fraulein Marshal to ride with her. A cavalier must keep his promise with a lady, at least till he knows she is ardently in love with him." He gave his hand to the duke, and as he left the room he hummed a light French chanson.

Ranuzi looked after him with a long, frowning glance. "Poor fool," murmured he, "he believes he plays his part so well that he deceives even me. This mask of folly and levity he has assumed is thin and transparent enough I see his true face behind it. It is the physiognomy of a sly intriguant. Oh, I know him thoroughly; I understand every emotion of his heart, and I know well what his passion for the beautiful Marshal signifies. She is the maid of honor of the Princess Henry this is the secret of his love. She is the confidante of the princess, who receives every week long and confidential letters from the tent of her tender husband. Fraulein Marshal is naturally acquainted with their contents. The prince certainly speaks in these letters of his love and devotion, but also a little of the king's plans of battle. Fraulein von Marshal knows all this. If Belleville obtains her love and confidence, he will receive pretty correct information of what goes on in the tent of the king and in the camp councils. So Belleville will have most important dispatches to forward to his Marquise de Pompadour dispatches for which he will be one day rewarded with honor and fortune. This is the Frenchman's plan! I see through him as I do through the Russian. They are both paid spies informers of their governments nothing more. They will be paid, or they will be hung, according as accident is favorable or unfavorable to them." Ranuzi was silent, and walked hastily backward and forward in the rood. Upon his high, pale brow dark thoughts were written, and flashes of anger flamed from his eyes.

"And I," said he, after a long pause, "am I in any respect better than they? Will not the day come when I also will be considered as a purchased spy? a miserable informer? and my name branded with this title? No, no; away with this dark spectre, which floats like a black cloud between me and my purpose! My aim is heaven; and what I do, I do in the name of the Church—in the service of this great, exalted Church, whose servant and priest I am. No, no; the world will not call me a spy, will not brand my name with shame. God will bless my efforts as the Holy Father in Rome has blessed them, and I shall reach the goal."

Ranuzi was brilliantly handsome in this inspired mood; his noble and characteristic face seemed illuminated and as beautiful as the angel of darkness, when surrounded by a halo of heavenly light.

"It is an exalted and great aim which I have set before me," said he, after another pause; "a work which the Holy Father himself confided to me. I must and I will accomplish it to the honor of God and the Holy Madonna. This blasphemous war must end; this atheistical and free-thinking king must be reduced, humbled, and cast down from the stage he has mounted with such ostentatious bravado. Silesia must be torn from the hands of this profligate robber and incorporated in the crown of our apostolic majesty of Austria. The holy Church dare not lose any of her provinces, and Silesia will be lost if it remains in the hands of this heretical king; he must be punished for his insolence and scoffing, for having dared to oppose himself to the Holy Father at Rome. The injuries which he heaped upon the Queen of Poland must be avenged, and I will not rest till he is so humbled, so crushed, as to sue for a shameful peace, even as Henry the Fourth, clad like a peasant, pleaded to Canoza. But the means, the means to attain this great object."

Hastily and silently he paced the room, his head proudly thrown back, and a cold, defiant glance directed upward.

"To kill him!" said he suddenly, as if answering the voices which whispered in his soul; "that would be an imbecile, miserable resort, and, moreover, we would not obtain our object; ho would not be humiliated, but a martyr's crown would be added to his laurels. When, however, ho is completely humbled, when, to this great victory at Hochkirch, we add new triumphs, when we have taken Silesia and revenged Saxony, then he might die; then we will seek a sure hand which understands the dagger and its uses. Until then, silence and caution; until then this contest must be carried on with every weapon which wisdom and craft can place in our hands. I think my weapons are good and sharp, well fitted to give a telling thrust; and yet they are so simple, so threadbare—a cunning fortune-teller, a love-sick fool, a noble coquette, and a poor prisoner! these are my only weapons, and with these I will defeat the man whom his flatterers call the heroic King of Prussia." He laughed aloud, but it was a ferocious, threatening laugh, which shocked himself.

"Down, down, ye evil spirits," said he; "do not press forward so boldly to my lips; they are consecrated now to soft words and tender sighs alone.

Silence, ye demons! creep back into my heart, and there, from some dark corner, you can hear and see if my great role is well played. It is time! it is time! I must once more prove my weapons."

He stepped to the glass and looked thoughtfully at his face, examined his eyes, his lips, to see if they betrayed the dark passions of his soul; then arranged his dark hair in soft, wavy lines over his brow; he rang for his servant, put on his Austrian uniform, and buckled on the sword. The king had been gracious enough to allow the captive officers in Berlin to wear their swords, only requiring their word of honor that they would never use them again in this war. When Count Ranuzi, the captive Austrian captain, had completed his toilet, he took his hat and entered the street. Ranuzi had now assumed a careless, indifferent expression; he greeted the acquaintances who met him with a friendly smile, uttering to each a few kindly words or gay jests. He reached, at last, a small and insignificant house in the Frederick Street, opened the door which was only slightly closed, and entered the hall; at the same moment a side door opened, and a lady sprang forward, with extended arms, to meet the count.

"Oh, my angel," said she, in that soft Italian tongue, so well suited to clothe love's trembling sighs in words—"oh, my angel, are you here at last? I saw your noble, handsome face, from my window; it seemed to me that my room was illuminated with glorious sunshine, and my heart and soul were warmed."

Ranuzi made no answer to these glowing words, silently he suffered himself to be led forward by the lady, then replied to her ardent assurances by a few cool, friendly words.

"You are alone to-day, Marietta," said he, "and your husband will not interrupt our conversation."

"My husband!" said she, reproachfully, "Taliazuchi is not my husband. I despise him; I know nothing of him; I am even willing that he should know I adore you."

"Oh woman, woman!" said Ranuzi, laughing; "how treacherous, how dangerous you are! When you love happily, you are like the anaconda, whose poisonous bite one need not fear, when it is well fed and tended, but when you have ceased to love, you are like the tigress who, rashly awaked from sleep, would strangle the unfortunate who disturbed her repose. Come, my anaconda, come; if you are satisfied with my love, let us talk and dream." He drew her tenderly toward him, and, kissing her fondly, seated her by his side; but Marietta glided softly to his feet.

"Let it be so," she said; "let me lie at your feet; let me adore you, and read in your face the history of these last three terrible days, in which I have not seen you. Where were you, Carlo? why have you forgotten me?"

"Ah," said he, laughing, "my anaconda begins to hunger for my heart's blood! how long before she will be ready to devour or to murder me?"

"Do not call me your anaconda," she said, shaking her head; "you say that, when we are satisfied with your love, we are like the sleeping anaconda. But, Carlo, when I look upon you, I thirst for your glances, your sweet words, your assurances of love. And has it not been thus all my life long? Have I not loved you since I was capable of thought and feeling? Oh, do you remember our happy, glorious childhood, Carlo? those days of sunshine, of fragrance, of flowers, of childish innocence? Do you remember how often we have wandered hand in hand through the Campagna, talking of God, of the stars, and of the flowers?—dreaming of the time in which the angels and the stars would float down into our hearts, and change the world into a paradise for us?"

"Ah! we had a bitter awaking from these fair dreams," said Ranuzi, thoughtfully. "My father placed me in a Jesuit college; your mother sent you to a cloister, that the nuns might make of you a public singer. We had both our own career to make, Marietta; you upon the stage, I on the confessor's stool. We were the poor children of poor parents, and every path was closed to us but one, the church and the stage; our wise parents knew this."

"And they separated us," sighed Marietta; "they crushed out the first modest flame of our young, pure hearts, and made us an example of their greed! Ah, Carlo; you can never know how much I suffered, how bitterly I wept on your account. I was only twelve years old, but I loved you with all the strength and ardor of a woman, and longed after you as after a lost paradise. The nuns taught me to sing; and when my clear, rich voice pealed through the church halls, no one knew that not God's image, but yours, was in my heart; that I was worshipping you with my hymns of praise and pious fervor. I knew that we were forever separated, could never belong to each other, so I prayed to God to lend swift wings to time, that we might become independent and free, I as a singer and you as my honored confessor."

Ranuzi laughed merrily. "But fate was unpropitious," said he. "The pious fathers discovered that I had too little eloquence to make a good priest; in short, that I was better fitted to serve holy mother Church upon the battle-field. When I was a man and sufficiently learned, they obtained a commission for me as officer in the Pope's body-guard, and I exchanged the black robe of my order for the gold-embroidered uniform."

"And you forgot me, Carlo? you did not let me know where you were? Five years after, when I was engaged in Florence as a singer, I learned what had become of you. I loved you always, Carlo; but what hope had I ever to tell you so? we were so far away from each other, and poverty separated us so widely. I must first become rich, you must make your career. Only then might we hope to belong to each other. I waited and was silent."

"You waited and were silent till you forgot me," said Ranuzi, playing carelessly with her long, soft curls; "and, having forgotten me, you discovered that Signer Taliazuchi was a tolerably pretty fellow, whom it was quite possible to love."

"Taliazuchi understood how to flatter my vanity," said she, gloomily; "he wrote beautiful and glowing poems in my praise, which were printed and read not only in Florence, but throughout all Italy. When he declared his love and pleaded for my hand, I thought, if I refused him, he would persecute me and hate me; that mockery and ridicule would take the place of the enthusiastic hymns in my praise, with which Italy then resounded. I was too ambitious to submit to this, and had not the courage to refuse him, so I became his wife, and in becoming so, I abhorred him, and I swore to make him atone for having forced me to become so."

"But this force consisted only in hymns of praise and favorable criticisms," said Ranuzi, quietly.

"I have kept my oath," said Marietta; "I have made him atone for what he has done, and I have often thought that, when afterward compelled to write poems in my favor, he cursed me in his heart; he would gladly have crushed me by his criticisms, but that my fame was a fountain of gold for him, which he dared not exhaust or dry up. But my voice had been injured by too much straining, and a veil soon fell upon it. I could but regard it as great good fortune when Count Algarotti proposed to me to take the second place as singer in Berlin; this promised to be more profitable, as the count carelessly offered Taliazuchi a place in the opera troupe as writer. So I left my beautiful Italy; I left you to amass gold in this cold north. And now, I no longer repent; I rejoice! I have found you again—you, the beloved of my youth—you, my youth itself. Oh, Heaven! never will I forget the day when I saw you passing. I knew you in spite of the uniform, in spite of the many years which had passed since we met. I knew you; and not my lips only, but my heart, uttered that loud cry which caused you to look up, my Carlo.

And now you recognized me and stretched your hands out to me, and I would have sprung to you from the window, had not Taliazuchi held me back. I cried out, 'It is Ranuzi! it is Carlo! I must, I will fly to him,' when the door opened and you entered and I saw you, my own beloved; I heard your dear voice, and never did one of God's poor creatures fall into a happier insensibility than I in that rapturous moment."

"And Taliazuchi stood by and smiled!" said Ranuzi, laughing; "it was truly a pretty scene for an opera writer. He, no doubt, thought so, and wished to take note of it, as he left the room when you awaked to consciousness."

"Since that time, I am only awake when in your presence," said Marietta, passionately. "When you are not near me, I sleep. You are the sun which rouses me to life. When you leave me, it is night—dark night, and dark, gloomy thoughts steal over me."

"What thoughts, Marietta?" said he, placing his hand under her chin, and raising her head gently.

She looked up at him with a curious, dreamy smile, but was silent.

"Well, what thoughts have you when I am not with you?" he repeated.

"I think it possible a day may come in which you will cease to love me."

"And you think you will then fly to Taliazuchi for consolation?" said Ranuzi, laughing.

"No; I think, or rather I fear that I will revenge myself; that I will take vengeance on you for your unfaithfulness."

"Ah! my tigress threatens!" cried Ranuzi. "Now, Marietta, you know well that I shall never cease to love you, but a day will come when we will be forced to separate." She sprang up with a wild cry, and clasped him stormily in her arms.

"No, no!" she cried, trembling and weeping; "no man shall dare to tear you from me! We will never be separated!"

"You think, then, that I am not only your prisoner for life, but also the eternal prisoner of the King of Prussia?"

"No, no! you shall be free—free! but Marietta will also be free, and by your side. When you leave Berlin, I go with you; no power can bind me here. Taliazuchi will not seek me, if I leave him my little fortune. I will do that; I will take nothing with me. Poor, without fortune or possessions, I will follow you, Ranuzi. I desire nothing, I hope for nothing, but to be by your side."

She clasped him in her arms, and did not remark the dark cloud which shadowed his brow, but this vanished quickly, and his countenance assumed a kind and clear expression. "It shall be so, Marietta! Freedom shall unite us both eternally, death only shall separate us! But when may we hope for this great, this glorious, this beautiful hour? When will the blessed day dawn in which I can take your hand and say to you, 'Come, Marietta, come; the world belongs to us and our love. Let us fly and enjoy our happiness.' Oh, beloved, if you truly love me, help me to snatch this happy day from fate! Stand by me with your love, that I may attain my freedom."

"Tell me what I can do, and it is done," said she resolutely; "there is nothing I will not undertake and dare for you."

Ranuzi took her small head in his hands and gazed long and smilingly into her glowing face.

"Are you sure of yourself?" said he.

"I am sure. Tell me, Carlo, what I must do, and it is done."

"And if it is dangerous, Marietta?"

"I know but one danger."

"What is that?"

"To lose your love, Carlo!"

"Then this world has no danger for you, Marietta!"

"Speak, Carlo, speak! How can I aid you? What can I do to obtain your liberty?"

Ranuzi threw a quick and searching glance around the room, as if to convince himself that they were alone, then bowed down close to her ear and whispered:

"I can never be free till the King of Prussia is completely conquered and subjected, and only if I bring all my strength and capabilities to this object, may I hope to be free, and rich, and honored. The King of Prussia is my enemy, he is the enemy of the Church, the enemy of my gracious sovereign of Austria, to whom I have sworn fealty. A man may strive to conquer his enemies with every weapon, even with craft. Will you stand by me in this?"

"I will."

"Then observe and listen, and search all around you. Repeat to me all that you hear and see—seem to be an enthusiastic adherent of the King of Prussia; you will then be confided in and know all that is taking place. Be kind and sympathetic to your husband; he is a sincere follower of the king, and has free intercourse with many distinguished persons; he is also well received at court. Give yourself the appearance of sympathizing in all his sentiments. When you attend the concerts at the castle, observe all that passes—every laugh, every glance, every indistinct word, and inform me of all. Do you understand, Marietta?—will you do this?"

"I understand, Carlo, and I will do this. Is this all? Can I do nothing more to help you?"

"Yes, there are other things, but they are more difficult, more dangerous."

"So much the better; the more dangerous the stronger the proof of my love. Speak, dear Carlo!"

"It is forbidden for the captive officers to send sealed letters to their friends or relatives. All our letters must be read, and if a word of politics is found in them, they are condemned. All other persons have the right to send sealed letters in every direction. Have you not friends to whom you write, Marietta?"

"I have, and from this time onward your friends will be mine, and I will correspond with them."

As she said this, with a roguish smile, a ray of joy lighted up Ranuzi's eyes.

"You understand me, my beloved; your intellect is as clear and sharp as your heart is warm and noble. Think well what you do—what danger threatens you. I tell you plainly, Marietta, this is no question of common friendly letters, but of the most earnest, grave, important interests!"

She bowed to his ear and whispered: "All that you espy in Berlin you will confide to these letters; you will concert with your friends, you will design plans, perhaps make conspiracies. I will address these letters and take them to the post, and no one will mistrust me, for my letters will be addressed to some friends in Vienna, or to whom you will. Have I understood you, Carlo? Is this all right?"

He clasped her rapturously in his arms, and the words of tender gratitude which he expressed were not entirely wanting in sincerity and truth.

Marietta was proudly happy, and listened with sparkling eyes to his honeyed words.

As Ranuzi, however, after this long interview, arose to say farewell, she held him back. Laying her hands upon his shoulder, she looked at him with a curious expression, half laughing, half threatening.

"One last word, Carlo," she said; "I love you boundlessly. To prove my love to you, I become a traitress to this king, who has been a gracious master to me, whose bread I eat—who received and protects me. To prove my love, I become a spy, an informer. Men say this is dishonorable work, but for myself I feel proud and happy to undertake it for you, and not for all the riches and treasures of this world would I betray you. But, Carlo, if you ever cease to love me, if you deceive me and become unfaithful, as true as God helps me, I will betray both myself and you!"

"I believe truly she is capable of it," said Ranuzi, as he reached the street; "she is a dangerous woman, and with her love and hate she is truly like a tigress. Well, I must be on my guard. If she rages I must draw her teeth, so that she cannot bite, or flee from her furious leaps. But this danger is in the distance, the principal thing is that I have opened a way to my correspondence, and that is immense progress in my plans, for which I might well show my gratitude to my tender Marietta by a few caresses."

CHAPTER IV
LOUISE DU TROUFFLE

Madame du Trouffle paced her room restlessly; she listened to every stroke of the clock, every sound made her tremble.

"He comes not! he comes not!" murmured she; "he received my irony of yesterday in earnest and is exasperated. Alas! am I really an old woman? Have I no longer the power to enchain, to attract? Can it be that I am old and ugly? No, no! I am but thirty-four years of age—that is not old for a married woman, and as to being ugly—"

She interrupted herself, stepped hastily to the glass, and looked long and curiously at her face.

Yes, yes! she must confess her beauty was on the wane. She was more faded than her age would justify. Already was seen around her mouth those yellow, treacherous lines which vanished years imprint upon the face; already her brow was marked with light lines, and silver threads glimmered in her hair.

Louise du Trouffle sighed heavily.

"I was too early married, and then unhappily married; at eighteen I was a mother. All this ages a woman—not the years but the storms of life have marked these fearful lines in my face. Then it is not possible for a man to feel any warm interest in me when he sees a grown-up daughter by my side, who will soon be my rival, and strive with me for the homage of men. This is indeed exasperating. Oh, my God! my God! a day may come in which I may be jealous of my own daughter! May Heaven guard me from that! Grant that I may see her fresh and blooming beauty without rancor; that I may think more of her happiness than my vanity."

Then, as if she would strengthen her good resolutions, Louise left her room and hastened to the chamber of her daughter.

Camilla lay upon the divan—her slender and beauteous form was wrapped in soft white drapery; her shining, soft dark hair fell around her rosy face and over her naked shoulders, with whose alabaster whiteness it contrasted strongly. Camilla was reading, and so entirely was she occupied with her book that she did not hear her mother enter.

Louise drew softly near the divan, and stood still, lost in admiration at this lovely, enchanting picture, this reposing Hebe.

"Camilla," said she, fondly, "what are you reading so eagerly?"

Camilla started and looked up suddenly, then laughed aloud.

"Ah, mamma," said she, in a silver, clear, and soft voice, "how you frightened me! I thought it was my tyrannical governess already returned from her walk, and that she had surprised me with this book."

"Without doubt she forbade you to read it," said her mother, gravely, stretching out her hand for the book, but Camilla drew it back suddenly.

"Yes, certainly, Madame Brunnen forbade me to read this book; but that is no reason, mamma, why you should take it away from me. It is to be hoped you will not play the stern tyrant against your poor Camilla."

"I wish to know what you are reading, Camilla."

"Well, then, Voltaire's 'Pucelle d' Orleans,' and I assure you, mamma, I am extremely pleased with it."

"Madame Brunnen was right to forbid you to read this book, and I also forbid it."

"And if I refuse to obey, mamma?"

"I will force you to obedience," cried her mother, sternly.

"Did any one succeed in forcing you to obey your mother?" said Camilla, in a transport of rage. "Did your mother give her consent to your elopement with the garden-boy? You chose your own path in life, and I will choose mine. I will no longer bear to be treated as a child—I am thirteen years old; you were not older when you had the affair with the garden-boy, and were forced to confide yourself to my father. Why do you wish in treat me as a little child, and keep me in leading-strings, when I am a grown-up girl?"

"You are no grown-up girl, Camilla," cried her mother; "if you were, you would not dare to speak to your mother as you have done: you would know that it was unseemly, and that, above all other things, you should show reverence and obedience to your mother. No, Camilla, God be thanked! you are but a foolish child, and therefore I forgive you."

Louise drew near her daughter and tried to clasp her tenderly in her arms, but Camilla struggled roughly against it.

"You shall not call me a child," said she, rudely. "I will no longer bear it! it angers me! and if you repeat it, mamma, I will declare to every one that I am sixteen years old!"

"And why will you say that, Camilla?"

Camilla looked up with a cunning smile.

"Why?" she repeated, "ah! you think I do not know why I must always remain a child? It is because you wish to remain a young woman—therefore you declare to all the world that I am but twelve years old! But no one believes you, mamma, not one believes you. The world laughs at you, but you do not see it—you think you are younger when you call me a child. I say to you I will not endure it! I will be a lady—I will adorn myself and go into society. I will not remain in the school-room with a governess while you are sparkling in the saloon and enchanting your followers by your beauty. I will also have my worshippers, who pay court to me; I will write and receive love-letters as other maidens do; I will carry on my own little love-affairs as all other girls do; as you did, from the time you were twelve years old, and still do!"

"Silence, Camilla! or I will make you feel that you are still a child!" cried Louise, raising her arm threateningly and approaching the divan.

"Would you strike me, mother?" said she, with trembling lips. "I counsel you not to do it. Raise your hand once more against me, but think of the consequences. I will run away! I will fly to my poor, dear father, whom you, unhappy one, have made a drunkard! I will remain with him—he loves me tenderly. If I were with him, he would no longer drink."

"Oh, my God, my God!" cried Louise, with tears gushing from her eyes; "it is he who has planted this hate in her heart—he has been the cause of all my wretchedness! She loves her father who has done nothing for her, and she hates her mother who has shown her nothing but love." With a loud cry of agony, she clasped her hands over her face and wept bitterly.

Camilla drew close to her, grasped her hands and pulled them forcibly from her face, then looked in her eyes passionately and scornfully. Camilla was indeed no longer a child. She stood erect, pale, and fiercely excited, opposite to her mother. Understanding and intellect flashed from her dark eyes. There were lines around her mouth which betrayed a passion and a power with which childhood has nothing to do.

"You say you have shown me nothing but love," said Camilla, in a cold and cutting tone. "Mother, what love have you shown me? You made my father wretched, and my childish years were spent under the curse of a most unhappy marriage. I have seen my father weep while you were laughing merrily—I have seen him drunk and lying like a beast at my feet, while you were in our gay saloon receiving and entertaining guests with cool unconcern. You say you have shown me nothing but love. You never loved me, mother, never! Had you loved me, you would have taken pity with my future—you would not have given me a step-father while I had a poor, dear father, who had nothing in the wide world but me, me alone! You think perhaps, mother, that I am not unhappy; while I am giddy and play foolish pranks, you believe me to be happy and contented. Ah, mother, I have an inward horror and prophetic fear of the future which never leaves me; it seems to me that evil spirits surround me—as if they enchanted me with strange, alluring songs. I know they will work my destruction, but I cannot withstand them—I must listen, I must succumb to them. I would gladly be different—be better. I desire to be a virtuous and modest girl, but alas, alas, I cannot escape from this magic circle to which my mother has condemned me! I have lived too fast, experienced too much—I am no longer a child—I am an experienced woman. The world and the things of the world call me with a thousand alluring voices, and I shall be lost as my mother was lost! I am her most unhappy daughter, and her blood is in my heart!" Almost insensible, crushed by excitement and passion, Camilla sank to the earth.

Her mother looked at her with cold and tearless eyes; her hair seemed to stand erect, and a cold, dead hand seemed placed upon her heart and almost stilled its beatings. "I have deserved this," murmured she; "God punishes the levity of my youth through my own child." She bowed down to her daughter and raised her softly in her arms.

"Come, my child," she said, tenderly, "we will forget this hour—we will strive to live in love and harmony with each other. You are right! You are no longer a child, and I will think of introducing you to the world."

"And you will dismiss Madame Brunnen," said Camilla, gayly. "Oh, mamma, you have no idea how she tortures and martyrs me with her Argus-eyes, and watches me day and night. Will you not dismiss her, mamma, and take no other governess?"

"I will think of it," said her mother, sadly. But now a servant entered and announced Count Ranuzi. Madame du Trouffle blushed, and directed the servant to conduct him to the parlor.

Camilla looked at her roguishly, and said: "If you really think me a grown-up girl, take me with you to the parlor."

Madame du Trouffle refused. "You are not properly dressed, and besides, I have important business with the count."

Camilla turned her back scornfully, and her mother left the room; Camilla returned to the sofa and Madame du Trouffle entered the saloon. In the levity and frivolity of their hearts they had both forgotten this sad scene in the drama of a demoralized family life; such scenes had been too often repeated to make any lasting impression.

Madame du Trouffle found Count Ranuzi awaiting her. He came forward with such a joyous greeting, that she was flattered, and gave him her hand with a gracious smile. She said triumphantly to herself that the power of her charms was not subdued, since the handsome and much admired Ranuzi was surely captivated by them.

The count had pleaded yesterday for an interview, and he had done this with so mysterious and melancholy a mien, that the gay and sportive Louise had called him the Knight of Toggenberg, and had asked him plaintively if he was coming to die at her feet.

"Possibly," he answered, with grave earnestness—"possibly, if you are cruel enough to refuse the request I prefer."

These words had occupied the thoughts of this vain coquette during the whole night; she was convinced that Ranuzi, ravished by her beauty, wished to make her a declaration, and she had been hesitating whether to reject or encourage him. As he advanced so gracefully and smilingly to meet her, she resolved to encourage him and make him forget the mockery of yesterday.

Possibly Ranuzi read this in her glance, but he did not regard it; he had attained his aim—the interview which he desired. "Madame," said he, "I come to make honorable amends, and to plead at your feet for pardon." He bowed on one knee, and looked up beseechingly.

Louise found that his languishing and at the same time glowing eyes were very beautiful, and she was entirely ready to be gracious, although she did not know the offence. "Stand up, count," said she, "and let us talk reasonably together. What have you done, and for what must I forgive you?"

"You annihilate me with your magnanimity," sighed Ranuzi. "You are so truly noble as to have forgotten my boldness of yesterday, and you choose to forget that the poor, imprisoned soldier, intoxicated by your beauty, carried away by your grace and amiability, has dared to love you and to confess it. But I swear to you, madame, I will never repeat this offence. The graceful mockery and keen wit with which you punished me yesterday has deeply moved me, and I assure you, madame, you have had more influence over me than any prude with her most eloquent sermon on virtue could have done. I have seen my crime, and never again will my lips dare to confess what lives and glows in my heart." He took her hand and kissed it most respectfully.

Louise was strangely surprised, and it seemed to her not at all necessary for the count to preserve so inviolable a silence as to his love; but she was obliged to appear pleased, and she did this with facility and grace.

"I thank you," she said, gayly, "that you have freed me from a lover whom, as the wife of Major du Trouffle, I should have been compelled to banish from my house. Now I dare give a pleasant, kindly welcome, to Count Ranuzi, and be ready at all times to serve him gladly."

Ranuzi looked steadily at her. "Will you truly do this?" said he, sighing—"will you interest yourself for a poor prisoner, who has no one to hear and sympathize in his sorrows?"

Louise gave him her hand. "Confide in me, sir count," said she, with an impulse of her better nature; "make known your sorrows, and be assured that I will take an interest in them. You are so prudent and reasonable as not to be my lover, and I will be your friend. Here is my hand—I offer you my friendship; will you accept, it?"

"Will I accept it?" said he, rapturously; "you offer me life, and ask if I will accept it!"

Louise smiled softly. She found that Ranuzi declared his friendship in almost as glowing terms as he had confessed his love. "So then," said she, "you have sorrows that you dare not name?"

"Yes, but they are not my own individual griefs I suffer, but it is for another."

"That sounds mysterious. For whom do you suffer?"

"For a poor prisoner, who, far from the world, far from the haunts of men, languishes in wretchedness and chains—whom not only men but God has forgotten, for He will not even send His minister Death to release him. I cannot, I dare not say more—it is not my secret, and I have sworn to disclose it to but one person."

"And this person—"

"Is the Princess Amelia of Prussia," said Ranuzi. Louise shrank back, and looked searchingly at the count. "A sister of the king! And you say that your secret relates to a poor prisoner?"

"I said so. Oh, my noble, magnanimous friend, do not ask me to say more; I dare not, but I entreat you to help me. I must speak with the princess. You are her confidante and friend, you alone can obtain me an interview."

"It is impossible! impossible!" cried Madame du Trouffle, rising up and pacing the room hastily. Ranuzi followed her with his eyes, observed every movement, and read in her countenance every emotion of her soul.

"I will succeed," said he to himself, and proud triumph swelled his heart.

Louise drew near and stood before him.

"Listen," said she, gravely; "it is a daring, a dangerous enterprise in which you wish to entangle me—doubly dangerous for me, as the king suspects me, and he would never forgive it if he should learn that I had dared to act against his commands, and to assist the Princess Amelia to save an unhappy wretch whom he had irretrievably condemned. I know well who this prisoner is, but do not call his name—it is dangerous to speak it, even to think it. I be long not to the confidantes of the princess in this matter, and I do not desire it. Speak no more of the prisoner, but of yourself. You wish to be presented to the princess. Why not apply to Baron Pollnitz?"

"I have not gold enough to bribe him; and, besides that, he is a babbler, and purchasable. To-morrow he would betray me."

"You are right; and he could not obtain you a secret interview. One of the maids of honor must always be present, and the princess is surrounded by many spies. But there is a means, and it lies in my hands. Listen!"

Louise bowed and whispered.

Ranuzi's face sparkled with triumph.

"To-morrow, then," said he, as he withdrew.

"To-morrow," said Louise, "expect me at the castle gate, and be punctual."

CHAPTER V
THE FORTUNE-TELLER

The heavy curtains were drawn down, and a gloomy twilight reigned in this great, silent room, whose dreary stillness was only interrupted by the monotonous stroke of the clock, and the deep sighs and lamentations which came from the sofa in a distant part of the room. There in the corner, drawn up convulsively and motionless, lay a female form, her hands clasped over her breast, her eyes fixed staringly toward heaven, and from time to time uttering words of grief and scorn and indignation.

She was alone in her anguish—ever alone; she had been alone for many years; grief and disappointment had hardened her heart, and made it insensible to all sorrows but her own. She hated men, she hated the world, she railed at those who were gay and happy, she had no pity for those who wept and mourned.

Had she not suffered more? Did she not still suffer? Who had been merciful, who had pitied her sorrows? Look now at this poor, groaning woman! Do you recognize these fearful features, deformed by sickness and grief; these blood-shot eyes, these thin, colorless lips, ever convulsively pressed together, as if to suppress a wild shriek of agony, which are only unclosed to utter cold, harsh words of scorn and passion? Do you know this woman? Has this poor, unhappy, deformed being any resemblance to the gay, beautiful, intellectual Princess Amelia, whom we once knew? and yet this is the Princess Amelia. How have the mighty fallen! Look at the transforming power of a few sorrowful years! The sister of a mighty hero king, but a poor desolate creature, shunned and avoided by all: she knows that men fly from her, and she will have it so; she will be alone—lonely in the midst of the world, even as he is, in the midst of his dark and gloomy prison. Amelia calls the whole world her prison; she often says to herself that her soul is shut in behind the iron bars of her body and can never be delivered, that her heart lies upon the burning gridiron of the base world, and cannot escape, it is bound there with the same chains which are around about and hold him in captivity.

But Amelia says this only to herself, she desires no sympathy, she knows no one will dare to pity her. Destiny placed her high in rank and alone—alone she will remain; her complaints might perhaps bring new danger to him she loves, of whom alone she thinks, for whose sake alone she supports existence, she lives only for him. Can this be called life? A perpetual hope—and yet hopeless—a constant watching and listening for one happy moment, which never comes! She had not been permitted to live for him, she would not die without him. So long as he lived he might need her aid, and might call upon her for help in the hour of extremest need, so she would not die.

She was not wholly dead, but her youth, her heart, her peace, her illusions, her hopes were dead; she was opposed to all that lived, to the world, to all mankind. In the wide world she loved but two persons: one, who languished in prison and who suffered for her sake, Frederick von Trenck; the other, he who had made her wretched and who had the power to liberate Trenck and restore their peace—the king. Amelia had loved her mother, but she was dead; grief at the lost battle of Collin killed her. She had loved her sister, the Margravine of Baireuth; but she died of despair at the lost battle of Hochkirch. Grief and the anger and contempt of the king had killed her brother, the Prince Augustus William of Prussia. She was therefore alone, alone! Her other sisters were far away; they were happy, and with the happy she had nothing to do; with them she had no sympathy. Her two brothers were in the field, they thought not of her. There was but one who remembered her, and he was under the earth—not dead, but buried—buried alive. The blackness of thick darkness is round about him, but he is not blind; there is glorious sunshine, but he sees it not.

These fearful thoughts had crushed Amelia's youth, her mind, her life; she stood like a desolate ruin under the wreck of the past. The rude storms of life whistled over her, and she laughed them to scorn; she had no more to fear—not she; if an oak fell, if a fair flower was crushed, her heart was glad; her own wretchedness had made her envious and malicious; perhaps she concealed her sympathy, under this seeming harshness; perhaps she gave herself the appearance of proud reserve, knowing that she was feared and avoided. Whoever drew near her was observed and suspected; the spies of the king surrounded her and kept her friends, if she had friends, far off. Perhaps Amelia would have been less unhappy if she had fled for shelter to Him who is the refuge of all hearts; if she had turned to her God in her anguish and despair. But she was not a pious believer, like the noble and patient Elizabeth Christine, the disdained wife of Frederick the Great.

Princess Amelia was the true sister of the king, the pupil of Voltaire; she mocked at the church and scorned the consolations of religion. She also was forced to pay some tribute to her sex; she failed in the strong, self-confident, intellectual independence of Frederick; her poor, weak, trembling hands wandered around seeking support; as religion, in its mighty mission, was rejected, she turned for consolation to superstition. While Elizabeth Christine prayed, Amelia tried her fortune with cards; while the queen gathered around her ministers of the gospel and pious scholars, the princess called to the prophets and fortune-tellers. While Elizabeth found comfort in reading the Holy Scriptures, Amelia found consolation in the mystical and enigmatical words of her sooth-sayers. While the queen translated sermons and pious hymns into French, Amelia wrote down carefully all the prophecies of her cards, her coffee-grounds, and the stars, and both ladies sent their manuscripts to the king.

Frederick received them both with a kindly and pitiful smile. The pious manuscript of the queen was laid aside unread, but the oracles of the princess were carefully looked over. Perhaps this was done in pity for the poor, wounded spirit which found distraction in such child's play. It is certain that when the king wrote to the princess, he thanked her for her manuscripts, and asked her to continue to send them. *[Footnote: Thiebault, p. 279.]* But he also demanded perfect silence as to this strange correspondence; he feared his enemies might falsely interpret his consideration for the weakness of the princess; they might suppose that he needed these prophecies to lead him on to victory, as his adversaries needed the consecrated sword.

This was one of the days on which the princess was accustomed to receive her fortune-teller; she had been very angry when told that she was under arrest; neither the prophet nor the fortune-teller were at liberty, and the princess was not able to obtain their release. She would, therefore, have been compelled to forego her usual occupation for the evening, had not Madame du Trouffle come to her aid. Louise had written that morning to the princess, and asked permission to introduce a new soothsayer, whose prophecies astonished the world, as, so far, they had been literally fulfilled. Amelia received this proposition joyfully, and now waited impatiently for Madame du Trouffle and the soothsayer; but she was yet alone, it was not necessary to hide her grief in stoical indifference, to still the groans of agony which, like the last sighs from a death-bed, rang from her breast.

The princess suffered not only from mental anguish; her body was as sick as her soul. The worm gnawing at her heart was also devouring her body; but neither for body nor soul would she accept a physician, she refused all sympathy for intellectual and physical pain. Amelia suffered and was silent, and only when as now she was certain there was no eye to see, no ear to hear her complaints, did she give utterance to them. And now the maid entered and announced Madame du Trouffle and the prophet.

"Let them enter," said the princess in a hollow, death-like voice; "let them enter, and remain yourself, Fraulein Lethow; the soothsayer shall tell your fortune."

The door opened, and Madame du Trouffle entered. She was gay and lovely as ever, and drew near the princess with a charming smile. Amelia returned her salutation coldly and carelessly.

"How many hours have you spent at your toilet to-day?" said she, roughly; "and where do you buy the rouge with which you have painted your cheeks?"

"Ah, your royal highness," said Louise, smiling, "Nature has been kind to me, and has painted my cheeks with her own sweet and cunning hand."

"Then Nature is in covenant with you, and helps you to deceive yourself to imagine that you are yet young. I am told that your daughter is grown up and wondrously beautiful, and that only when you stand near her is it seen how old and ugly you are."

Louise knew the rancor of the unhappy princess, and she knew no one could approach her without being wounded — that the undying worm in her soul was only satisfied with the blood it caused to flow. The harsh words of the princess had no sting for her. "If I were truly old," said she, "I would live in my daughter: she is said to be my image, and when she is praised, I feel myself flattered."

"A day will come when she will be blamed and you will also be reproached," murmured Amelia. After a pause she said: "So you have brought me another deceiver who declares himself a prophet?"

"I do not believe him to be an impostor, your highness. He has given me convincing proofs of his inspiration."

"What sort of proofs? How can these people who prophesy of the future prove that they are inspired?"

"He has not told me of the future, but of the past," said Louise.

"Has he had the courage to recall any portion of your past to you?" said the princess, with a coarse laugh.

"Many droll and merry portions, your highness, and it is to be regretted that they were all true," she said, with comic pathos.

"Bring in this soothsayer, Fraulein von Lethow. He shall prophesy of you: I think you have not, like Madame du Trouffle, any reason to fear a picture of your past."

The prophet entered. He was wrapped in a long black robe, which was gathered around his slender form by a black leathern girdle covered with curious and strange figures and emblems; raven black hair fell around his small, pale face; his eyes burned with clouded fire, and flashed quickly around the room. With head erect and proud bearing, he drew near the princess, and only when very near did he salute her, and in a sweet, soft, melodious voice, asked why she wished to see him.

"If you are truly a prophet, you will know my reasons."

"Would you learn of the past?" said he, solemnly.

"And why not first of the future?"

"Because your highness distrusts me and would prove me. Will you permit me to take my cards? If you allow it, I will first prophesy to this lady." He took a mass of soiled, curiously painted cards, and spread them out before him on the table. He took the hand of Fraulein Lethow and seemed to read it earnestly; and now, in a low, musical voice, he related little incidents of the past. They were piquant little anecdotes which had been secretly whispered at the court, but which no one dared to speak aloud, as Fraulein Lethow passed for a model of virtue and piety.

She received these developments of the prophet with visible scorn. In place of laughing, and by smiling indifference bringing their truth in question, she was excited and angry, and thus prepared for the princess some gay and happy moments.

"I dare not decide," said Amelia, as the prophet ceased, "whether what you have told is true or false. Fraulein Lethow alone can know that; but she will not be so cruel as to call you an impostor, for that would prevent me from having my fortune told. Allow me, therefore, to believe that you have spoken the truth. Now take your cards and shuffle them."

"Does your highness wish that I should tell you of the past?" said the soothsayer, in a sharp voice.

The princess hesitated. "Yes," said she, "of my past. But no; I will first hear a little chapter out of the life of my chaste and modest Louise. Now, now, madame, you have nothing to fear; you are pure and innocent, and this little recitation of your by-gone days will seem to us a chapter from 'La Pucelle d'Orleans.'"

"I dare to oppose myself to this lecture," said Louise, laughing. "There are books which should only be read in solitude, and to that class belong the volumes of my past life. I am ready in the presence of your highness to have my future prophesied, but of my past I will hear nothing—I know too much already."

"Had I been alone with Fraulein Lethow, I should have told her many other things, and she would have been forced to believe in my power. Only when these cards are under your eyes is my spirit clear."

"I must, then, in order to know the whole truth from you, be entirely alone?" said the princess.

The prophet bowed silently. Amelia fixed a piercing glance upon him, and nodded to her ladies.

"Go into the next room," said she. "And now," said the princess, "you can begin."

The magician, instead of taking the cards, knelt before the princess and kissed the hem of her robe. "I pray for mercy and forgiveness," said he; "I am nothing but a poor impostor! In order to reach the presence of your royal highness, I have disguised myself under this mask, which alone made it possible. But I swear to you, princess, no one knows of this attempt, no one can ever know it—I alone am guilty. Pardon, then, princess—pardon for this bold act. I was forced to this step—forced to clasp your knees—to implore you in your greatness and magnanimity, to stand by me! I was impelled irresistibly, for I had sworn a fearful oath to do this thing."

"To whom have you sworn?" said the princess, sternly. "Who are you? what do you ask of me?"

"I am Count Ranuzi, Austrian captain and prisoner of war. I implore you, noble princess, to have mercy upon a poor, helpless prisoner, consumed with grief and despair. God and the world have forsaken him, but he has one protecting angel in whom he trusts, to whom he prays—and her name is Amelia! He is bound in chains like a wild beast—a hard stone is his couch, and a vault beneath is his grave—he is living and buried—his heart lives and heaves and calls to you, princess, for rescue."

The Princess Amelia shrank back trembling and groaning on the sofa; her eyes were wide open, and staring in the distance. After a long pause, she said, slowly: "Call his name."

"Frederick von Trenck!"

Amelia shuddered, and uttered a low cry. "Trenck!" repeated she, softly; "oh, what sad melody lies in that word! It is like the death-cry of my youth. I think the very air must weep when this name vibrates upon it. Trenck, Trenck! How beautiful, how lovely that sounds; it is a sweet, harmonious song; it sings to me softly of the only happiness of my life. Ah, how long, how long since this song was silenced! All within me is desolate! On every side my heart is torn—on every side! Oh, so drear, so fearful! All!

all!" Lost in her own thoughts, these words had been slowly uttered. She had forgotten that she was not alone with her remembrances, which like a cloud had gathered round about her and shut off the outward world.

Ranuzi did not dare to recall her thoughts—he still knelt at her feet.

Suddenly her whole frame trembled, and she sprang up. "My God! I dream, while he calls me! I am idly musing, and Trenck has need of me. Speak, sir, speak! What do you know of him? Have you seen him? Did he send you to me?"

"He sent me, your highness, but I have not seen him. Have the grace to listen to me. Ah, your highness, in what I now say I lay the safety of a dear and valued friend, yes, his life, at your feet. One word from you, and he will be delivered over to a court-martial and be shot. But you will not speak that word—you are an angel of mercy."

"Speak, sir—speak, sir," said Amelia, breathlessly. "My God! do you not see that I am dying from agitation?"

"Princess, Trenck lives—he is in chains—he is in a hole under the earth—but he lives, and as long as he has life, he hopes in you—has wild dreams of liberty, and his friends think and hope with him. Trenck has friends who are ready to offer up their lives for him. One of them is in the fortress of Magdeburg—he is lieutenant of the guard; another is a Captain Kimsky, prisoner of war; I am a third. I have known Trenck since my youth. In our beautiful days of mirth and revelry, we swore to stand by each other in every danger. The moment has come to fulfil my oath—Trenck is a prisoner, and I must help to liberate him. Our numbers are few and dismembered—we need allies in the fortress, and still more in the city. We need powerful assistance, and no one but your highness can obtain it for us."

"I have an assured and confidential friend in Magdeburg," said the princess; "at a hint from me he will be ready to stand by you to—"

Suddenly she was silent, and cast a searching, threatening glance at Ranuzi. She had been too often deceived and circumvented—snares had been too often laid at her feet—she was distrustful. "No, no," said she, at last, sternly, rudely—"I will take no part in this folly. Go, sir—go. You are a poor soothsayer, and I will have nothing to do with you."

Ranuzi smiled, and drew a folded paper from his bosom, which he handed to the princess. It contained these words: "Count Ranuzi is an honest man—he can be trusted unconditionally." Under these words was written: "Nel tue giorni felici, vicordati da me."

The breast of Amelia heaved convulsively—she gazed at these written characters; at last her eyes filled with tears—at last her heart was overcome by those painful and passionate feelings which she had so long kept in bondage. She pressed the paper, the lines on which were written with his blood, to her lips, and hot tears gushed from those poor eyes which for long, long years, had lost the power to weep.

"Now, sir," said she, "I believe in you, I trust you. Tell me what I have to do."

"Three things fail us, princess: A house in Magdeburg, where Trenck's friends can meet at all hours, and make all necessary preparations, and where he can be concealed after his escape. Secondly, a few reliable and confiding friends, who will unite with us and aid us. Thirdly, we must have gold—we must bribe the guard, we must buy horses, we must buy friends in the fortress, and lastly, we must buy French clothing. Besides this, I must have permission to go for a few days to Magdeburg, and there on the spot I can better make the final preparations. A fair pretext shall not fail me for this; Captain Kimsky is my near relative—he will be taken suddenly ill, and as a dying request he will beg to see me; one of his comrades will bring me notice of this, and I will turn imploringly to your highness."

"I will obtain you a passport," said Amelia, decisively.

"While in Magdeburg, the flight will be arranged."

"And you believe you will succeed?" said the princess, with a bright smile, which illuminated her poor deformed visage with a golden ray of hope.

"I do not only believe it, I know it; that is, if your royal highness will assist us."

The princess made no reply; she stepped to her desk and took from it several rolls of gold, then seated herself and wrote with a swift hand: "You must trust the bearer fully, he is my friend; assist him in all that he undertakes." She folded the paper and sealed it.

Ranuzi followed every movement with flashing eyes and loudly beating heart. As she took the pen to write the address a ray of wild triumph lighted his dark face, and a proud smile played about his mouth. As Amelia turned, all this disappeared, and he was dignified and grave as before.

"Take this, sir," said she; "you see that I place in your power a faithful and beloved friend, he is lost if you are false. As soon as you reach Magdeburg go to him, and he will make other friends and allies known to you."

"Can I make use of this address, and write under it to my friend Kimsky?" said Ranuzi. "Yes, without danger. To-day I will find means to inform him that he may expect this letter. Here is gold, two hundred ducats, all that I have at present. When this is exhausted, turn again to me and I will again supply you."

Ranuzi took the gold and said, smilingly, "This is the magic means by which we will break his chains."

Amelia took a costly diamond pin, which lay upon the table, and gave it to Ranuzi. She pointed to the paper marked with blood, which she still held in her hand.

"This is a most precious jewel which you have given me—let us exchange."

Ranuzi fell upon his knees and kissed her hand as ho took the pin.

"And now, sir, go. My maid is a salaried spy, and a longer interview would make you suspected. You would be watched, and all discovered. Go! If I believed in the power of prayer, I would lie upon my knees night and day, and pray for God's blessing upon your effort. As it is, I can only follow you with my thoughts and hopes. Farewell!"

"Your royal highness sends no reply to these lines, written with Trenck's heart's blood?"

Amelia took the pen and wrote a few hasty lines upon the paper, which she handed Ranuzi. The words were: "Ovunque tu sei vicina ti sono."

"Give him that," said she; "it is not written with my heart's blood, but my heart bleeds for him—bleeds ever inwardly. And now resume your role of soothsayer—I must call my ladies."

The afternoon of this day Ranuzi wrote to his friend, Captain Kimsky, prisoner of war at Magdeburg: "The train is laid, and will succeed. The fortress will soon be in our hands. A romantic, sentimental woman's heart is a good thing, easily moved to intrigues. Magdeburg will be ours! Prepare everything—be ill, and call for me; I shall get a passport. I have a powerful protectress, and with such, you know, a man mar attain all the desires of his heart!"

CHAPTER VI
A COURT DAY IN BERLIN

It was the birthday of Prince Henry, and was to be celebrated with great pomp at the court. The king had himself written explicitly on this subject to the master of ceremonies, Baron Pollnitz. Pollnitz was, therefore, actively occupied in the early morning, and no general ever made his preparations for a battle with more earnestness and importance than the good baron gave his orders for the splendid fete which was to be given in the royal apartments that night.

And this was indeed a great opportunity. The people of Berlin were to enjoy a ball and a concert, at which all the Italian singers were to be present; and then a rare and costly supper, to which not only the court, but all the officers who were prisoners of war were to be invited.

This supper was to Pollnitz the great circumstance, the middle point of the fete. Such an entertainment was now rare at the court of Berlin, and many months might pass away ere the queen would think of giving another supper. Pollnitz knew that when he thirsted now for a luxurious meal he must enjoy it at his own cost, and this thought made him shudder. The worthy baron was at the same time a spendthrift and a miser.

Four times in every year he had three or four days of rare and rich enjoyment; he lived en grand seigneur, and prepared for himself every earthly luxury; these were the first three or four days of every quarter in which he received his salary. With a lavish hand he scattered all the gold which he could keep back from his greedy creditors, and felt himself young, rich, and happy. After these fleeting days of proud glory came months of sad economy; he was obliged to play the role of a parasitical plant, attach himself to some firm, well-rooted stem, and absorb its strength and muscle. In these days of restraint he watched like a pirate all those who were in the condition to keep a good table, and so soon as he learned that a dinner was on hand, he knew how to conquer a place. At these times he was also a passionate devotee of the card-table, and it was the greatest proof of his versatility and dexterity that he always succeeded in making up his party, though every man knew it cost gold to play cards with Pollnitz. The grand-master had the exalted principles of Louis XV. of France, who was also devoted to cards. Every evening the great Louis set apart a thousand louis d'or to win or lose. If the king won, the gold went into his private pocket; if he lost, the state treasury suffered.

Following this royal example, Pollnitz placed the gold he won in his pocket; if he lost, he borrowed the money to pay—he considered this borrowed sum as also the clear profit of his game; he was assured to win, and in this way he obtained his pocket money.

To-day, however, he would not be merry at a strange table; he himself would do the honors, and he had conducted the arrangements of the table with a scholarship and knowledge of details which would have obtained the admiration of the Duke de Richelieu.

On this occasion it was not necessary to restrain his luxurious desires and tastes. Honor demanded that the court should show itself in full pomp and splendor, and prove to the world that this long, wearisome war had not exhausted the royal treasury, nor the royal table service of silver; in short, that it was an easy thing to carry on the war, without resorting to the private treasures of the royal house.

It was, therefore, necessary to bring out for this great occasion the golden service which had been the king's inheritance from his mother. Frederick's portion had been lately increased by the death of the Margravino of Baireuth, who had explicitly willed her part to her brother Frederick. *[Footnote: When the court fled, after the battle of Kunendorf, to Magdeburg, they took the golden service which the king inherited from his mother with them; that portion given to Frederick by the margravino was left in Berlin, and the next year, 1760, was seized by the Russians and carried to Petersburg—"Geschichte Berlins," vol. v., p. 2.]*

The queen and the princesses were to appear in all the splendor of their jewels, and by their costly and exquisite toilets impose upon these proud and haughty officers, whom fate had sent as prisoners of war to Berlin, and who would not fail to inform their respective governments of all they saw in the capital.

This fete was a demonstration made by the king to his over-confident enemies. He would prove to them that if he wished for peace it was not because the gold failed to carry on the war, but because he wished to give rest and the opportunity to recover to Europe, groaning and bleeding from a thousand wounds. Besides this, the king wished to show his subjects, by the celebration of his brother's birthday, how highly he honored the prince— how gladly he embraced the opportunity to distinguish the young general who, during the whole war, had not lost a single battle; but, by his bold and masterly movements, had come to the king's help in the most difficult and dangerous moments.

This celebration should be a refutation of the rumors spread abroad by the king's enemies, that Frederick regarded the success and military talent of his brother with jealous envy.

There were, therefore, many reasons why Pollnitz should make this a luxurious and dazzling feast; he knew also that Prince Henry would receive a detailed account of the celebration from his adjutant, Count Kalkreuth, who had lingered some months in Berlin because of his wounds, was now fully restored, and would leave Berlin the morning after the ball to return to the army.

And now the important hour had arrived. Pollnitz wandered through the saloons with the searching glance of a warrior on the field of battle; he pronounced that all was good.

The saloons were dazzling with light; pomp and splendor reigned throughout, and on entering the supper-room you were almost blinded by the array of gold and silver adorning the costly buffet, on whose glittering surface the lights were a thousand times reflected.

Suddenly the rooms began to fill; everywhere gold-embroidered uniforms, orders, stars, and flashing gems were to be seen; a promiscuous and strange crowd was moving through these lofty saloons, illuminated by thousands of lights and odorous with the fragrance of flowers.

Side by side with the rich, fantastic uniform of the Russian, was seen the light and active French chasseur; here was to be seen the Hungarian hussar, whose variegated and tasteful costume contrasted curiously with the dark and simple uniform of the Spaniard, who stood near him, both conversing gayly with an Italian, dressed in the white coat of an Austrian officer.

It seemed as if every nation in Europe had arranged a rendezvous for this day in the royal palace at Berlin, or as it the great Frederick had sent specimens to his people of all the various nations against whom he had undertaken this gigantic war.

There were not only Germans from all the provinces, but Italians, Spaniards, Russians, Swedes, Hungarians, Netherlanders, and Frenchmen. All these were prisoners of war—their swords had been stained with the blood of Prussians; the fate of war now confined them to the scabbard, and changed the enemies of the king into guests at his court.

Hundreds of captive officers were now waiting in the saloon for the appearance of the queen, but the Prussian army was scarcely represented.

All who were fit for service were in the field, only the invalids and the old warriors, too infirm for active duty had remained at the capital; even the youths who had not attained the legal age for military duty, had hastened to the army, full of courage and enthusiasm, inspired by the example of their fathers and brothers.

The dazzling appearance of these royal saloons was therefore mostly owing to the flashing uniforms of the prisoners of war. Only a few old Prussian generals, and the courtiers, whose duties prevented them from being heroes, were added to the number.

Herr von Giurgenow, and his friend Captain Belleville, were invited to the ball, and were well pleased to offer their homage to the majesty of Prussia. Count Ranuzi, who, reserved and silent as usual, had been wandering through the saloons, now joined them, and they had all withdrawn to a window, in order to observe quietly and undisturbed the gay crowd passing before them.

"Look you," said Ranuzi, laughing, "this reminds me of the frantic confusion in the anterooms of hell, which Dante has described in such masterly style. We all wear our glittering masks, under which our corpses are hidden; one word from our master and this drapery would fall off, and these grinning death-heads be brought to ruin. It depends solely upon the will of Frederick of Prussia to speak this word. He is our master, and when he commands it, we must lay aside our swords and exchange our uniforms for the garments of a malefactor."

"He will not dare to do this," said Giurgenow; "all Europe would call him a barbarian, and make him answerable for his insolence."

"First, all Europe must be in a condition to call him to account," said Ranuzi, laughing; "and that is certainly not the case at present, I am sorry to say."

"You have not heard, then," said Belleville, "of the glorious victory which our great General Broglie has gained over Duke Ferdinand of Brunswick; all France is jubilant over this happy event, and the Marquise de Pompadour, or rather King Louis, has made this second Turenne, our noble Broglie, marshal."

"I know of this," said Ranuzi; "but I know also that the fortune of battles is inconstant, otherwise we would not now be here."

"It is to be hoped we will not be here long," said Giurgenow, impatiently. "Does it not lie in our power to go at once? What think you? Have we not our swords? They have not dared to take them from us! They tremble before us, and honor, in our persons, the nations we represent.

Look at the complaisance and consideration with which we are met on all sides. The King of Prussia fears his powerful enemies, and does all in his power to conciliate them. Suppose that to-night, as soon as the royal family are assembled, we draw our swords and take them all prisoners; we have overpowering numbers, and I think it would be an easy victory. We could make a fortress of this palace, and defend ourselves; they would not dare to make a violent attack, as the queen and princesses would be in our power. What think you of this plan, Count Ranuzi?"

Ranuzi met the sharp and piercing glance of the Russian with cool composure.

"I think it bold, but impossible. We could not maintain our position, one hour. The garrison of Berlin would overcome us. We have no thousands of prisoners in the casements here, as in Kustrin, to aid us in such an attempt."

"The count is right," said Belleville, gayly; "such a grandiose and warlike conspiracy would amount to nothing. We must revenge ourselves in another way for the tedious ennui we are made to endure here, and my friends and myself are resolved to do so. We will no longer submit to the shackles of etiquette, which are laid upon us; we will be free from the wearisome constraint which hems us in on every side. These proud ladies wish us to believe that they are modest and virtuous, because they are stiff and ceremonious. They make a grimace at every equivoque. We will prove to them that we are not blinded by this outward seeming, and not disposed to lie like Dutchmen, languishing at the feet of our inexorable fair ones. Our brave brothers have conquered the Prussians at Hochkirch and at Bergen; we cannot stand side by side with them in the field, but here, at least, we can humble the Prussian women!"

"I can well believe," whispered Giurgenow, "that you would be pleased to humble the beautiful Fraulein von Marshal?"

"Ah, my friend," said Ranuzi, laughing, "you touch the wound of our poor friend. You do not seem to know that the beautiful Marshal is responsible for the scorn and rage of Count Belleville, she is indeed a haughty and presumptuous beauty; she not only dared to reject the love of the fascinating count, but she showed him the door; and when afterward he ventured to send her a passionate and tender billet-doux, she informed him, through her servant, that she would give the letter to her chambermaid, for whom, without doubt, it was intended."

"Eh bien, what do you say to this insolence?" cried the enraged Frenchman. "But she shall do penance for it. I have already made the necessary arrangements with my friends. This is not simply a personal affair, it touches the general honor. The whole French army, all France, is insulted in my person. It is necessary we should have satisfaction, not only from this presumptuous lady, but from all the ladies of the court! We will have our revenge this evening! We will show to these dull dames what we think of their prudery. And the queen shall see that we are not at all inclined to bow down to her stiff ceremonies. She is, in our eyes, not a queen—simply the wife of an enemy over whom we will soon triumph gloriously."

"I counsel you, however, to wait till the hour of triumph for your revenge," said Ranuzi. "Your intentions may lead to the worst consequences for us all. The great Frederick will never be a harmless adversary till he is dead, and we would all be ignominiously punished for any contempt shown the queen. You have a personal affair with Fraulein Marshal; well, then, you must make her personally responsible; but do not involve us all in your difficulties. It would be an easy thing to forfeit even this appearance of freedom."

"You are right," said Giurgenow; "we might be banished from Berlin, and that would be a bitter punishment for us all."

"But look! the doors are being thrown open, and the queen and court will appear; you will have the happiness of seeing your cruel fair one," whispered Ranuzi to the Frenchman.

"I assure you she shall repent of her cruelty to-night," said Belleville, gnashing his teeth. Exchanging a significant glance with several French officers, who were standing not far off, he advanced into the saloon to the outer circle, which was formed on both sides, and through which the queen and court must pass.

Now the grand master of ceremonies appeared on the threshold, with his golden staff. Behind him the queen and the Princess Amelia entered the room; both appeared in all the pomp and splendor of their rank. A small diamond-crown glittered in the blonde hair of the queen, a magnificent necklace of diamonds and emeralds was clasped around her dazzlingly white and beautifully formed throat.

Bielfeld had once declared that this necklace could purchase a kingdom. A white robe worked with silver and a dark-red velvet shawl trimmed with ermine fell in graceful folds around the noble and graceful figure of the queen, whose bowed head, and quiet, modest bearing contrasted strangely with the luxury and splendor which surrounded her.

Another striking contrast to the queen was offered in the presence of the Princess Amelia. Like her royal sister, she appeared in complete toilet, adorned with all her jewels—her arms, her throat, her hair, and her hands flashed with diamonds. The festoons of her robe of silver gauze were fastened up with diamond buttons, and beneath appeared a green robe embroidered with silver. The princess knew full well that all this splendor of toilet, all these flashing gems, would bring into contemptuous notice her sharp, angular figure, and her poor deformed visage; she knew that the eyes of all would be fixed upon her in derision, that her appearance alone would be greeted as a cherished source of amusement, and as soon as her back was turned the whole court would laugh merrily. She assumed, as usual, a cold contemptuous bearing; she met mockery with mockery, and revenged herself by sharp wit and cutting irony for the derisive glances which plainly spoke what the lips dared not utter. She no sooner entered the saloon than she began to greet her acquaintances; every word contained a poisonous sting, which inflicted a grievous wound. When she read in the faces of her victims that her sharp arrows had entered the quivering flesh, a malicious fire sparkled in her eyes, and a bitter smile played upon her lips.

Behind the queen and Princess Amelia appeared the Princess Henry. She was also superbly dressed, but those who looked upon her thought not of her toilet; they were refreshed, enraptured by her adorable beauty—by the goodness and purity written on her rosy cheek. To-day, however, the eyes of the princesses were less clear and dazzling than usual—a gleam of sadness shadowed her fair brow, and her coral lips trembled lightly as if in pain. Perhaps it was the remembrance of the beautiful and happy days, past and gone like a dream, which made the lonely present seem so bitter. Absentminded and thoughtful, she stepped forward without looking to the right or left, regardless of the flashing orders and stars, of the handsome officers and courtly circle bowing profoundly before her as she passed on.

The court had now passed; the bowed heads were raised, and now the young French officers cast impertinent, almost challenging glances, at the ladies of the queen and the princesses, who drew near and bestowed here and there stolen smiles and light greetings upon their admirers.

Fraulein Marshal did not seem to be aware that the insolent eyes of these haughty Frenchmen were fixed upon her. Proudly erect she advanced; her large blue eyes were turned toward the princess; she gave neither glance nor smile to any one; her noble and beautiful countenance had a stern, resolved expression—her lips were pouting, and her usually soft eyes told tales of an angry soul. There was something Juno-like in her appearance— she was lovely to behold, but cold and stern in her beauty.

As she passed by Count Belleville, he exclaimed with a sigh to his neighbor: "Ah, look at this majestic Galatea, this beautiful marble statue, which can only be awaked to life by kisses."

Fraulein Marshal trembled slightly; a crimson blush suffused her face, her shoulders, and even her back; but she did not hesitate or turn. She moved on slowly, though she heard the officers laughing and whispering—though she felt that their presumptuous eyes were fixed upon her.

The queen and princesses made the grande tournee through the rooms, and then mingled with the guests; all formal etiquette was now laid aside, and a gay and unembarrassed conversation might be carried on till the beginning of the concert. This seemed to degenerate, on the part of the French officers, to an indiscreet, frenzied levity. They laughed and talked boisterously—they walked arm in arm before the ladies, and remarked upon them so boldly, that crimson blushes, or frightened pallor, was the result. Even the queen remarked the strange and unaccountable excitement of her guests, and to put an end to it, she entered the concert-room and ordered the music to commence. Even this had no effect. The royal capello played an overture composed by the king, with masterly precision—the singers emulated them in an Italian aria—but all this did not silence the noisy conversation of the Frenchmen. They laughed and chatted without restraint; and neither the amazed glances of the princesses nor the signs of the grand-master of ceremonies, made the slightest impression upon them.

Suddenly there was a slight pause, and the Princess Amelia rose up from her seat and beckoned with her fan to Baron Pollnitz. In a loud and angry voice, she said: "Baron Pollnitz, I insist upon your forcing these shrieking popinjays of the Marquise de Pompadour to silence. We cannot hear the music for their loud chattering. The like birds may pass very well in the gallant boudoir of a certain marquise, but not in a royal palace of Berlin."

Pollnitz shrank back in alarm, and fixed an imploring look upon the princess. Amongst the French officers arose an angry murmur, swelling louder and louder, more and more threatening, and completely drowning the music which was just recommencing.

The queen bowed down to the princess. "I pray you, sister," said she in a low voice, "remember that we are poor, unprotected women, and not in a condition to defend ourselves. Let us appear not to remark this unmannerly conduct, and let us remember that the king has made it our duty to receive the French officers with marked attention."

"You, sister, are simply a slave to the commands of the king. He is more truly your master than your husband," said the princess, angrily.

The queen smiled sweetly. "You are right; I am his slave, and my soul has chosen him for its lord. Blame me not, then, for my obedience."

"Do you intend to allow the arrogant presumption of these haughty Frenchmen to go unpunished?"

"I will take pains not to observe it," said the queen, turning her attention again to the music. During all this time, Count Belleville stood behind Fraulein Marshal. While the concert was going on, he bowed over her and spoke long and impressively. Fraulein Marshal did not reply; neither his ardent love-assurances, nor his glowing reproaches, nor his passionate entreaties, nor his bold and offensive insolence, could draw from her one word, one look.

When the concert was over, and they were about to return to the saloon where, until supper, they could dance and amuse themselves, the young maiden turned with calm composure and indifference to Count Belleville. "Sir, I forbid you to molest me with your presence, and I counsel you no longer to offend my ears with these indecent romances, which you have no doubt learned upon the streets of Paris. But if, believing that I am unprotected, you still dare to insult me, I Inform you that my father has this moment arrived, and will certainly relieve me from your disagreeable and troublesome society." She spoke aloud, and not only Belleville, but the group of French officers who stood behind him, heard every word. She passed by them with calm indifference and joined a large, elderly officer, who was leaning against a pillar, and who stretched out his hand smilingly toward her.

"Father," she said, "God himself put it in your heart to come to Berlin this day. You are by my side, and I have nothing to fear. I know you can protect me."

In the mean time, the musicians commenced to play the grave and at the same time coquettish minuet, and the officers drew near the ladies to lead them to the dance. This was done, however, in so bold and unconstrained a manner, with such manifest nonchalance, the request was made with such levity, the words were so little respectful, that the ladies drew back frightened. Princess Amelia called Fraulein Marshal to her side. She took her hand with a kindly smile.

"My child," she said, "I rejoice that you have the courage to defy these shameless coxcombs. Go on, and count upon my protection. Why are you not dancing?"

"Because no one has asked me."

At this moment an officer drew near with diligent haste, apparently to lead her to the dance. While in the act of offering his hand to her he made a sudden movement, as if he had just recognized the lady, turned his back, and withdrew without a word of apology.

The princess was enraged. "I promise you they shall be punished for this presumption." She turned to Baron Marshal, who stood behind his daughter: "Baron," said she, "if this leads to a duel, I will be your second!"

CHAPTER VII
IN THE WINDOW-NICHE

While these events were occurring in the dancing-room, and the queen was seated at the card-table, the Princess Wilhelmina, wife of Prince Henry, stood in the window-niche of the ball-room and conversed with Count Kalkreuth, the friend and adjutant of her husband. The count had been sent home amongst the wounded, but he was now restored and about to return to the camp. They spoke quickly and impressively together, but the music drowned their words and made them indistinct to all others. What said they to each other? Seemingly petty and indifferent things. They had, perhaps, a deeper, secret meaning, for the countenance of the princess and that of the count were grave, and the sweet smile had vanished from the charming face of the princess. They spoke of unimportant things, perhaps, because they had not the courage for the great word which must be spoken—the word farewell!

"Your royal highness has then no further commission to give me for the prince?" said the count, after a pause.

"No," said the princess; "I wrote to him yesterday by the courier. Describe the ball to him, and tell him how we are, and how you left me."

"I must tell him, then, that your highness is perfectly gay, entirely happy, and glowing with health and beauty," said the count. These were simple and suitable words, but they were spoken in a hard and bitter tone.

The princess fixed her large soft eyes with an almost pleading expression upon the count; then with a quick movement she took a wreath of white roses, which she wore in her bosom, and held them toward him. "As a proof that I am gay and happy," said she, "take these flowers to my husband, and tell him I adorned myself with them in honor of his fete."

The count pressed his lips convulsively together and looked angrily upon the princess, but he did not raise his hand to take the flowers—did not appear to see that she held them toward him.

"Well, sir," said the Princess Wilhelmina, "you do not take the flowers?"

"No," said he, passionately, "I will not take them." The princess looked anxiously around; she feared some one might have heard this stormy "No." She soon convinced herself that there was no listener nearer than her maid of honor; Fraulein Marshal was still near the Princess Amelia, and she was somewhat isolated by etiquette; she saw, therefore, that she dared carry on this conversation.

"Why will you not take my flowers?" she said, proudly.

The count drew nearer. "I will tell you, princess," said he—"I will tell you, if this passionate pain now burning in my breast does not slay me. I will not take your flowers, because I will not be a messenger of love between you and the prince; because I cannot accept the shame and degradation which such an office would lay upon me. Princess you have forgotten, but I remember there was a wondrous time in which I, and not the prince, was favored with a like precious gift. At that time you allowed me to hope that this glowing, inextinguishable feeling which filled my heart, my soul, found an echo in your breast; that at least you would not condemn me to die unheard, misunderstood."

"I knew not at that time that my husband loved me," murmured the princess; "I thought I was free and justified in giving that heart which no one claimed to whom I would."

"You had no sooner learned that the prince loved you than you turned from me, proud and cold," said the count, bitterly; "relentlessly, without mercy, without pity, you trampled my heart under your feet, and not a glance, not a word showed me that you had any remembrance of the past. I will tell you what I suffered. You have a cold heart, it will make you happy to hear of any anguish. I loved you so madly I almost hated you; in the madness of my passion I cursed you. I thanked God for the war, which forced me to that for which I had never found the moral strength to leave you. Yes, I was grateful when the war called me to the field—I hoped to die. I did not wish to dishonor my name by suicide. I was recklessly brave, because I despised life—I rushed madly into the ranks of the enemy, seeking death at their hands, but God's blessed minister disdained me even as you had done. I was borne alive from the battle-field and brought to Berlin to be nursed and kindly cared for. No one knew that here I received daily new and bitter wounds. You were always cruel, cruel even to the last moment; you saw my sufferings, but you were inexorable. Oh, princess, it would have been better to refuse me entrance, to banish me from your presence, than to make my heart torpid under the influence of your cold glance, your polished speech, which ever allured me and yet kept me at a distance. You have played a cruel game with me, princess you mock me to the last. Shall I be your messenger to the prince? You know well that I would give my heart's blood for one of those sweet flowers, and you send them by me to another. My humility, my subjection is at an end; you have sinned against me as a woman, and I have therefore the right to accuse you as a man. I will not take these flowers! I will not give them to the prince! And now I have finished—I beg you to dismiss me."

The princess had listened tremblingly; her face became ever paler—completely exhausted, she leaned against the wall.

"Before you go," whispered she, "listen to a few words; it may be that the death you seek may be found on the battle-field—this may be our last interview in this world; in such a moment we dare speak the truth to each other; from the souls which have been closely veiled, may cloud and darkness be for one moment lifted. What I now say to you shall go as a sacred secret with you to the grave, if you fall; but if God hears my prayer, and you return, I command you to forget it, never to remind me of it. You say I have a cold heart. Alas! I only choked the flame which raged within me; I would have my honor and my duty burned to ashes. You say that my eyes are never clouded, that they shed no tears. Ah! believe me, I have wept inwardly, and the silent, unseen tears the heart weeps are bitterer than all others. You reproach me for having received you when you returned here sick and wounded, and for not having closed my doors against you. I know well that was my duty, and a thousand times I have prayed to God on my knees for strength to do this, but He did not hear me or He had no mercy. I could not send you off; had my lips spoken the fearful words, the shriek of my heart would have called you back. My lips had strength to refuse an answer to the question which I read in your face, in your deep dejection, but my heart answered you in silence and tears. Like you, I could not forget— like you I remembered the bounteous sweet past. Now you know all— go! As you will not take these flowers to the prince, they are yours, were intended for you; I have baptized them with my tears. Farewell!"

She gave him the flowers, and without looking toward him, without giving him time to answer, she stepped forward and called her chamberlain.

"Count Saldow, be kind enough to accompany Count Kalkreuth, and give him the books and papers my husband has ordered."

Wilhelmina passed on proudly, calmly, with a smile on her lips, but no one knew what it cost her poor heart. She did not look back. Kalkreuth would have given years to take leave once more of the lovely face, to ask pardon for the hard, rude words he had dared to say. The princess had still the bashful timidity of virtue; after the confession she had made she dared not look upon him. The count controlled himself; he followed Saldow. He was bewildered, rapturously giddy. As he left the castle and entered his carriage he looked up at the window and said: "I will not die!—I will return!"—then pressed the bouquet to his lips and sank back in the carriage.

CHAPTER VIII
THE NUTSHELLS BEHIND THE FAUTEUIL OF THE QUEEN

Princess Wilhelmina, as we have said, did not look back; she stepped silently through the ball-room, and approached the Princess Amelia. She stood for a moment behind a couple who were dancing the Francaise. The French officers had just taught this dance to the Prussian ladies as the newest Parisian mode.

It was a graceful and coquettish dance, approaching and avoiding; the ladies stood opposite their cavaliers, and advanced with smiling grace, then appeared to fly from them in mocking haste. They were pursued in artistic tours by their cavaliers; at the end of the dance their hands were clasped in each other's, and they danced through the room with the graceful time and step of the minuet.

Princess Wilhelmina stood silent and unobservant; she knew not the dance was ended; she knew not that the music was silenced. A softer, sweeter, dearer melody sounded in her ears; she heard the echo of that voice which had spoken scornfully, despairingly, and yet love had been the sweet theme.

The sudden stillness waked her from her dream and she stepped forward. The general silence was interrupted by the well-known coarse, stern voice of the Princess Amelia.

"Does this dance please you, Baron Marshal? The French officers have taught it to our ladies as a return for the dance which our brave Prussian soldiers taught the French at Rossbach; at Rossbach, however, they danced to a quicker, faster tempo. These Frenchmen are now calling out, 'En avant!' but at Rossbach, I am told, 'En arriere!' was the word of command."

A death-like silence followed these sarcastic words of the princess, and throughout the room her mocking, derisive laugh which followed these words was distinctly heard. She rose, and leaning upon the arm of Baron Marshal, advanced to meet the Princess Wilhelmina, and cast a fierce glance at the officers, who were assembled in groups and talking in low tones but earnestly with each other.

Suddenly Belleville, leaning on another officer, advanced from one of these groups; they walked backward and forward, laughing and chattering loudly, without regarding the presence of the princess. They then drew near the orchestra, and called out in a jovial tone:

"Messieurs, have the kindness to play a Dutch waltz, but in the quick time which the Austrians played at Hochkirch, when they drove the Prussians before them; and in which Field-Marshal Broglie played at Bergen, when he tramped upon the Prussians! Play on, messieurs! play on!"

Belleville then danced forward with great levity of manner to Fraulein Marshal, who stood by the side of her father; without saluting her, he seized her hand.

"Come, ma toute belle," said he, "you have played the marble statue long enough for one day; it is time that you should awake to life in my arms. Come, then, and dance with me your lascivious Dutch waltz, which no respectable woman in France would dare to dance! Come! come!"

Belleville tried to drag Fraulein Marshal forward, but at the instant a powerful and heavy arm was laid upon him, and his hand was dashed off rudely.

"I have heard you to the end," said Baron Marshal, calmly; "I wished to see a little of the renowned gallantry of which the Frenchman is so proud. It appears to me that a strange ton must now reign in Paris, well suited, perhaps, to the boudoirs of mistresses, but not fitting or acceptable to the ears of respectable women. I beg you therefore, sir, not to assume this ton in Berlin; I am resolved not to endure it."

Belleville laughed aloud, drew very near the baron, and looked him insolently in the face.

"Who are you, monsieur, who dare take the liberty of begging me, who do not know you, to do or not do any thing?"

"I am Baron Marshal, the father of this lady whom you have dared to offend!"

Belleville laughed still louder than before.

"Aha! that is a beautiful fairy tale! You who are as hideous as a baboon, and have borrowed the eyes of the cat!—you the father of the lovely Galatea Marshal!—tell that tale to other ears—I do not believe in such aberrations of Nature. I repeat my question: who are you? what is your name?"

"I repeat to you, I am Baron Marshal, the father of this lady."

"You are more credulous, sir, than I am, if you believe that," said Belleville, coarsely.

"Perhaps I am less credulous than you suppose," said Marshal, quietly. "It would, for example, be difficult for me to believe that you are a nobleman. I can assure you, however, that I am not only noble, but a man of honor."

Belleville was in the act of giving a passionate answer, when the doors of the supper-room were thrown open, and a sea of light irradiated the room.

At this moment, the queen and her ladies entered from the card-room, and, at her appearance, every word, every sound was hushed. Silently, and with a conciliatory smile, the queen passed through the saloon, and seated herself at the table; she then gave the sign to the grand-master, that her guests should be seated. And now the servants, in golden liveries, flew from side to side bearing silver plates, containing the rare and fragrant viands which the inventive head of Baron Pollnitz had ordered for the favored guests of her majesty the Queen of Prussia.

Nothing is so well calculated to quiet the perturbed soul as a costly and well-prepared feast. The haughty Frenchmen soon forgot their mortified vanity and resentment, and were well pleased to be seated at the table of the "great Frederick." They ate and drank right merrily in honor of the bold and brave prince who had sent them here from Rossbach; but if the rich dishes made them forget their mortification, the fiery wine excited yet more their presumptuous levity. They forgot that they were the guests of a queen. Louder and more extravagant was their gayety, more boisterous, more indiscreet their unrestrained laughter. In their frantic merriment they dared to sing aloud some of the little ambiguous, equivocal chansons, which belonged to the gamins of Paris, and at which the Marquise de Pompadour laughed till she shed tears when sung sometimes by the merry courtiers.

In vain the grand-master besought them, in his most polished manner, not to sing at table.

"We have been so long forced to listen to the dull, screeching discord of your singers, that we must have some compensation!" said they. "Besides," said Belleville, in a loud voice, "it belongs now to bon ton to sing at the table; and the Prussian court should thank us for introducing this new Parisian mode."

They sang, chatted, laughed, and almost overpowered the music by their boisterous levity. Their presumptuous revelry seemed to be every moment on the increase. The Austrian and Russian officers looked upon them with disgust and alarm, and entreated them to desist; but the French officers were regardless of all etiquette. During the dessert, Belleville and some of his friends arose and drew near the table at which the queen and the princesses were seated; this was in the middle of the room, and slightly separated from the other tables. They gazed at the princesses with insolent eyes, and, placing themselves behind the chair of the queen, they began to crack nuts with their teeth, and throw the shells carelessly upon the floor, near her majesty.

The queen continued a quiet conversation with the Princess Wilhelmina, and appeared wholly unconscious of this rudeness and vulgarity; but her face was pallid, and her eyes filled with tears.

"I pray your majesty to rise from the table!" said the Princess Wilhelmina. "Look at the Princess Amelia; her countenance glows with anger; there is a tempest on her brow, and it is about to burst upon us."

"You are right; that is the best way to end this torture." She rose from the table, and gave a sign for a general movement. When the queen and her suite had left the room, Baron Marshal drew near Count Belleville.

"Sir." said he. "I told you before that I was not sufficiently credulous to take you for a nobleman. Your conduct at the table has proved that I did well to doubt you. Yourself and friends have shown that you are strangers to the duties of cavaliers, and utterly ignorant of the manners of good society."

"Ah!" cried Belleville, "this offence demands satisfaction."

"I am ready to grant it," said Baron Marshal; "name the time and place of meeting."

"You know well," cried Belleville, "that I am a prisoner, and have given my word of honor not to use my sword!"

"So you were impertinent and shameless, because you knew you were safe? You knew that, thanks to your word of honor, you could not be chastised!"

"Sir," cried Belleville, "you forget that you speak not only to a nobleman, but to a soldier."

"Well, I know that I speak to a Frenchman, who lost his powder-mantle and pomatum-pot at Rossbach."

Belleville, beside himself with rage, seized his sword, and half drew it from the scabbard.

"God be praised, I have a sword with which to revenge insult!" he cried. "I have given my word not to use it on the battle-field against the Prussians, but here we stand as private adversaries, man to man, and I challenge you, sir—I challenge you to mortal combat. I will have satisfaction! You have insulted me as a nobleman, as a Frenchman, and as a soldier. No consideration shall restrain me. I dare not use my sword—well, then, we will fight with pistols. As to time and place, expect me to-morrow, at eight o'clock, in the Thiergarden."

"I accept the conditions, and I will await you with your seconds," said Baron Marshal.

"If the baron has not chosen his seconds," said a soft voice behind him, "I beg to offer my services."

Baron Marshal turned, and saw an officer in the Austrian uniform.

"Count Ranuzi," cried Belleville, astonished; "how, monsieur! you offer yourself as second to my adversary? I had thought to ask this service of you."

"I suspected so," said Ranuzi, with his accustomed calm and quiet manner, "therefore I anticipated you. The right is certainly on the side of Baron Marshal, and in offering myself as his second. I do so in the name of all the Austrian officers who are present. They have all seen the events of this evening with painful indignation. Without doubt the world will soon be acquainted with them; we wish to make an open, public demonstration that we wholly disapprove the conduct of the French officers. The nutshells thrown behind the fauteuil of the queen have made us your adversaries, Count Belleville."

"That is not the occasion of this duel, but the affront offered me by Baron Marshal," cried Belleville. "This being the case, will you still be the second of my opponent?"

"I was compelled to insult you," said Baron Marshal, "because you would have given me no satisfaction for the nutshells thrown behind the fauteuil of the queen; but be assured that I don't fight with you in order that you may wash out my offence with my blood, but wholly and alone that your blood may wash away the nutshells from the feet of the queen."

Baron Marshal then turned to Ranuzi. "I accept your offer, sir, and rejoice to make the acquaintance of a true nobleman. Have the goodness to meet the seconds of Count Belleville, and make all necessary arrangements. I will call for you early in the morning. I only say further that it is useless to make any attempts at reconciliation—I shall not listen to them. Prussia and France are at war. My great king has made no peace—I also will not hear of it. The nutshells lie behind the fauteuil of the queen, and only the blood of Count Belleville can wash them away."

He bowed to Ranuzi, and joined his daughter, who, pale and trembling, awaited him in the next room.

"Oh, father," said she, with tears gushing from her eyes, "your life is in danger—you meet death on my account!"

"No, thank God, my child, your name will not be mixed up in this affair. No one can say that the mortified father revenged an insult offered to his daughter. I fight this duel not for you, but because of the nutshells behind the fauteuil of the queen."

CHAPTER IX
THE DUEL AND ITS CONSEQUENCES

Early in the morning two horsemen dashed down the Linden. Their loud conversation, their pert and noisy laughter, aroused the curiosity of the porters who stood yawning in the house-doors, and the maids opened the windows and gazed curiously at the two gallant French officers who were taking such an early ride to the Thiergarden. When the girls were young and pretty, Belleville threw them a kiss as he passed by, and commanded them to give it with his tenderest greeting to their fair mistress.

"Happily," said his companion, "these good Berliners do not understand our speech sufficiently to inform their mistresses of this last insolence of Count Belleville."

"They do not, but their mistresses do, and I cannot think that they are still sleeping. No, I am convinced they have risen early, and are now standing behind their maids, and watching us go by. In this street dwell those who call themselves society; they were at the castle yesterday, and know of this duel. I think our good marquise will one day reward me richly for this duel, when I tell her I stood behind the queen and cracked nuts like a gamin in Paris, and that I was shot at because of the nutshells. She will laugh tears—tears which I will strive to convert into diamonds for myself."

"You feel assured that you will return unharmed from this duel?"

"Yes, I cannot doubt it. I always won the prize at our pistol-shooting in Paris, and then, this stupid Dutchman is, without doubt, horrified at the thought of shooting at a man, and not at a mark. No, vraiment, I do not doubt but I shall be victorious, and I rejoice in anticipation of that dejeuner dinatoire with which my friends will celebrate it."

"But," said his second, "let us for a moment suppose that you are not victorious; one must ever be prepared in this poor world, ruled by accident, for the worst that can befall. In case you fall, have you no last commissions to give me?"

Count Belleville stopped his horse as they were in the act of entering the garden.

"You positively insist on burying me? Well, then. I will make my last will. In case I fall go instantly to my quarters, open my writing-desk, and press upon a small button you will see on the left side; there you will find letters and papers; tie them carefully, and send them in the usual way to Countess Bernis. As to my heritage, you know I have no gold; I leave nothing but debts My clothes you can give to my faithful servant, Francois; for the last year I have paid him no wages Now my testament is made—no, stop, I had forgotten the most important item. Should the inconceivable, the unimaginable happen, should this Dutch village—devil slay me, I make it the duty of the French officers here to revenge me on the haughty daughter of my adversary, and on all these dull and prudish beauties. They must carry out what I intended yesterday. I have drawn a few sketches and added a few notes; make as many copies as are required, and paste them on the designated places. If I fall, this must be done the following night, that my wandering soul may find repose in the sweet consciousness of revenge. If my enemy's ball strikes me, hasten forward, and, before any one dares lay his hand upon me, take from my breast-pocket a paper, which you will find there, and conceal it; it is the drawing, and it is my legacy to my comrades. Swear to me to do as I have said."

"I swear!"

"And now, mon ami, let us forget this stupid thought of death, and look life saucily and merrily in the face. Life will not have the courage to break with a brave son of la belle France."

Belleville drew his bridle suddenly, and sprang through the gate into the garden; turning to the right, they rode for some time under the shadow of the trees, then through a side allee, which led to an open place surrounded by lofty oaks. At this moment he heard the roll of an open carriage, and turning, he saluted gayly the two gentlemen who were seated in it; he checked his horse suddenly in order to ride by their side, and provoking the beautiful and noble beast by the rude use of his spurs, he forced it into many difficult and artistic evolutions. Arrived at the place of rendezvous, he sprang lightly from the saddle and fastened his horse to a tree, then drew near Baron Marshal, who, with Ranuzi, was just descending from the carriage.

"No man could be more prudent than yourself, sir," said he, laughing, "to come to a rendezvous in a carriage; truly, that is a wise and, I think on this occasion, well-grounded precaution."

"A forethought which I have exercised on your account," said the baron, gravely. "You, sir, will require a carriage, and knowing you, as a stranger, had no carriage in Berlin, I brought mine. It shall be at your service."

"Vraiment! you are too good! I hope, however, not to make use of your offer."

Now, according to custom, Ranuzi drew near the baron to make a last attempt at reconciliation. He answered sternly: "You know that I am not to blame, and therefore will take no step in this matter. I suppose, Count Belleville is as little disposed as myself to make apologies."

"I intend to prove to you, sir baron, that I am a nobleman and a brave one; and as to the nuts which I cracked behind the queen, my only regret is, that they, like every thing else in your detested Berlin, were hollow—"

"No, sir, they were not at all hollow," said Baron Marshal, drawing up the cock of his pistol; "in one of those nuts I saw a death-worm, which will soon bore into your flesh."

He bowed to Belleville and took the place pointed out by his second. The second of Belleville then drew near, and led him to the outermost point of the line.

The Frenchman laughed aloud. "How," said he, "you will take me to the end of the world to secure me from the ball of my enemy?"

"Sir," said the grave and solemn voice of the baron, "you will still be too near me."

"Well, sir baron, I give you precedence," said Belleville, laughing, "though, I believe, I have the right; but age must have the precedence—fire, sir."

"No, young man," said Marshal, sadly; "I will grant you one more glance at the glad sun and the fresh, green earth; you shall fire first, and I council you to lay aside your levity; let your hand be firm and your aim steady; if you fail, you are lost. I am a good shot, and I am without mercy."

There was something so convincing, so gloomy in his tone, that Belleville was involuntarily affected by it. For the first time his brow was clouded, and a slight pallor took possession of his cheek; but he forced back this prophetic shudder quickly, and raised his pistol with a firm hand.

Far away, in the still park, sounded the echo of his shot; but opposite to him stood his adversary, firm and calm as before, with his eye fixed steadily upon him.

Belleville threw his pistol to the ground, and drawing his gold snuff-box from his vest-pocket with his small white hands, adorned with cuffs of lace, he played carelessly upon the lid; then opened it, and slowly and gracefully took a pinch of snuff, saying, coolly, "I await your ball."

Marshal raised his pistol and aimed directly at the head of his enemy, who looked him firmly in the eye. The appearance of this youthful, fresh, and brave face softened, against his will, the noble and magnanimous soul of this good man. He let his arm fall. "Sir," said he, "you are so young, perhaps your life may improve. I will not kill you. But you need for this life a great, impressive lesson and a lasting warning. I will therefore shoot you through the right leg, just above the knee." [Footnote: The words of Baron Marshal. — See Thiebault.] He raised the pistol quickly, and fired. As the smoke was lifted, Belleville was seen lying bleeding on the ground. The shot had gone right through the knee and broken the knee-pan.

As his second bowed over him, Belleville whispered, with broken eyes and trembling lips: "My legacy! do not forget my legacy! I believe I shall die; this pain is horrible."

The Frenchman took the paper from his pocket and concealed it "I will be avenged," said Belleville, with a convulsive smile, then sank into unconsciousness.

Belleville was placed in the carriage of Baron Marshal and carried to the city. Baron Marshal went immediately to the commandant of Berlin, gave notice of what had taken place, and declared himself under arrest.

The commandant took his hand kindly. "The laws forbid duelling, and I must consider you under arrest until I receive further orders. That is to say, house-arrest; you must give me your word not to leave your house. I will send a courier immediately to the king. I was in the castle last night, and witness to all the circumstances which led to this duel, witnessed the conduct of these Frenchmen, and in your place I would have acted just as you have done."

The French officers fulfilled the vow they had made to their wounded comrade; they had promised to revenge him on Fraulein Marshal and the other ladies of the court.

The morning after the duel, on the corners of all the principal streets, placards were pasted, which were soon surrounded by crowds of men, exhibiting astonishment and indignation. These placards contained a register of all the young and beautiful women of the court and city; to these names were added a frivolous and voluptuous personal description of every lady, and to this the name of the French officer which each was supposed to favor. [Footnote: Thiebault, p. 90.]

An outcry of scorn and rage was heard throughout Berlin; every one was excited at the boundless shamelessness of the French officers, and on this occasion the mass of the people took the part of the rich and the distinguished, whom generally they envied and despised. They felt themselves aggrieved by the contempt and ridicule which these Frenchmen had cast upon the daughters of Prussians, and no police force was necessary to tear these placards from the walls; they were torn off and trampled under foot, or torn into a thousand pieces and scattered to the winds. If a Frenchman dared to show himself on the street, he was received with curses and threats, and the police were obliged to forbid them to appear in any public place, as they feared they would not be able to protect them from the fierce indignation of the people. The doors of all the prominent houses, in which heretofore they had received so much attention, were now closed against them. The commandant of Berlin had sent a detailed account of the conduct of the French officers to the king, and the answer had been received.

Eight days after the placards had been pasted up by the Frenchmen, exactly upon the same places new placards were to be found, around which the people were again assembled; on every face was seen a happy smile, from every lip was heard expressions of harmony and approbation. This was a greeting of the king not only to his Berliners, but to Prussia and to the world; he was now "the Great Frederick," and all Europe listened when he spake. Frederick's greeting read thus:

"It is known to all Europe that I have provided every possible comfort to all officers who are prisoners of war. Swedes, Frenchmen, Russians, Austrians I have allowed to pass the time of their captivity at my capital. Many among them have taken advantage of the confidence reposed in them and carried on a forbidden correspondence; they have also, by unmannerly and presumptuous conduct, greatly abused the privileges allowed them; I therefore feel myself constrained to send them to Spandau, which city must not be confounded with the fortress of the same name at Spandau; they will be no more restricted than in Berlin, but they will be more closely watched."

"For this decision I cannot be blamed. The law of nations and the example of my allied enemies justify me fully. The Austrians have not allowed any of my officers who have fallen into their hands to go to Vienna. The Russians have sent their captives to Kasan. My enemies lose no opportunity to give a false aspect to my acts; I have, therefore, thought it wise to make known the causes which lead me to change my policy with regard to the prisoners of war."

"FREDERICK."

Two of the officers, with whom we are acquainted, were not included in this sentence of banishment.

One was Count Belleville. On the day that his comrades, deprived of their swords, left Berlin, his corpse was carried through the outer gate.

The shot of Baron Marshal made an amputation necessary, and death was the consequence. While his friends, whose condemnation he had brought about, marched sadly to Spandau, his body was laid in the "Friedhof." To the corpse had been granted a favor denied to the living—his sword was allowed to deck his coffin.

The Austrian officer, Ranuzi, because of his wise and prudent conduct and the powerful support he gave to Baron Marshal, was permitted to remain in Berlin. Ranuzi received this permission with triumphant joy. As he looked from his window at the prisoners marching toward Spandau, he said with a proud smile—"It is written, 'Be wise as a serpent.' These fools have not regarded the words of Holy Writ, and therefore they are punished, while I shall be rewarded. Yes, my work will succeed! God gives me a visible blessing. Patience, then, patience! A day will come when I will take vengeance on this haughty enemy of the Church. On that day the colors of the apostolic majesty of Austria shall be planted on the fortress of Magdeburg!"

CHAPTER X
THE FIVE COURIERS

It was the morning of the thirteenth of August. The streets of Berlin were quiet and empty. Here and there might be seen a workman with his axe upon his shoulder, or a tradesman stepping slowly to his comptoir. The upper circle of Berlin still slumbered and refreshed itself after the emotions and excitements of yesterday.

Yesterday had been a day of rejoicing; it had brought the news of the great and glorious victory which the crown prince, Ferdinand of Brunswick, had gained at Minden, over the French army under Broglie and Contades.

The crown prince had ever remembered that great moment in the beginning of the war, when his mother took leave of him in the presence of the Brunswick regiments. Embracing him for the last time, she said: "I forbid you to appear before me till you have performed deeds of valor worthy of your birth and your allies!" *[Footnote: Bodman.]*

Her son, the worthy nephew of Frederick the Great had now bought the right to appear before his mother.

By the victories of Gotsfeld and Minden he had now wiped out the defeat at Bergen, and the laurels which Brissac had won there were now withered and dead.

Berlin had just received this joyful news. After so much sorrow, so much humiliation and disappointment, she might now indulge herself in a day of festal joy, and, by public declarations and testimonials, make known to the world how dear to her heart was this victory of her king and his generals, and how deep and warm was the sympathy she felt.

All work was set aside in honor of this great celebration—the people were spread abroad in the meadows and woods, shouting and rejoicing, playing and dancing; the rich and the distinguished joined them without ceremony, to prove to the world that in such great moments, all differences of rank were forgotten—that they were all members of one body—united in joy and in sorrow by an electric chain.

So they slumbered on; the streets were still empty, the windows still closed.

But see! There comes a horseman through the Frankfort gate, dusty and breathless; his glowing face was radiant with joy! As he dashed through the streets he waved a white handkerchief high in the air, and with a loud and powerful voice, cried out, "Victory! victory!"

This one word had a magic influence. The windows flew up, the doors were dashed open, and shouting and screaming crowds of men rushed after the horseman. At a corner they surrounded his horse and compelled him to stop. "Who is victorious?" cried they tumultuously.

"The king—the great Frederick! He has whipped the Russians at Kunersdorf!"

A cry of rapture burst from every lip. "The king is victorious! he has defeated the Russians!"

Onward flew the courier to the palace; after him streamed the mad people. "The days of mourning are over—the blood of our sons has not been shed in vain, they are the honored dead—their death brought victory to the fatherland; they have drenched the soil with the blood of our barbarous enemies. We whipped the French at Minden, the Russians at Kunersdorf, and now we have defeated the Austrians and won back the trophies of their victory at Hochkirch!"

The people surrounded the castle shouting and triumphing. The courier had entered to give to the queen the joyful news. Soon the royal messengers were flying into every corner of the city to summon the ministers and officers of state to the castle. On foot, on horseback, in carriages, they hastened on, and the people received them with joyful shouts. "The king is victorious; the Russians are defeated!"

And now a door opened on a balcony, and Minister Herzberg stepped out. He waved his hat joyfully high in the air. The people returned this greeting with a roar like an exulting lion. He waved his hand, and the lion ceased to roar—there was death-like silence. He then told them that the king had offered battle to the Russians, yesterday, not far from Frankfort. The Russian army was greatly superior in numbers; they received the Prussians with a fearful, deadly fire! Unrestrainable, regardless of cannon-balls, or of death, the Prussians rushed on, stormed all the strongholds, and drove the Russian militia with fearful slaughter back to the graveyard of Kunersdorf. At five o'clock the king sent off the courier and the victory was assured.

"The victory was assured!" reechoed the mighty voice of the people. With warm and kindly eyes they looked upon each other. Proud, glad, happy, men who did not know each other, who had never met, now felt that they were brothers, the sons of one fatherland, and they clasped hands, and shouted their congratulations.

Suddenly, at the end of the street, another horseman appeared. He drew nearer and nearer. It is a second courier, a second message of our king to his family and his Berliners.

The people looked at him distrustfully, anxiously. What means this second courier? What news does he bring?

His countenance gay, his brow clear, with a flashing smile he greets the people. He brings news of victory—complete, assured victory.

Like the first courier, he dashed on to the castle, to give his dispatches to the queen and the ministers. The people were drunk with joy. The equipages of the nobles rolled by. Every one whose rank gave him the privilege wished to offer his personal congratulations to the queen.

And now in the Konigstrasse was seen a venerable procession. The magistrates of Berlin—in front the burgomasters with their long periwigs and golden chains, behind them the worthy city council—all hastened to the castle to offer congratulations in the name of the city.

The crowd drew back respectfully before the worthy city fathers, and opened a path for them, then fixed their eyes again upon the balcony where Minister Herrberg again appeared, and called for silence.

He will give us the news of the second courier. The victory is absolute. The Russians completely defeated. They had retreated to Kunersdorf. In this village they proposed to defend themselves. But the Prussians were unceasingly pressing upon them. Seven redoubts, Kirchhof, Spitzberg, and one hundred and eighty-six cannon had been taken. The enemy had suffered a monstrous loss, and was in the greatest confusion. The fate of the day seemed conclusive. This was owing to the heroic courage of the army, whom neither the blazing heat of the sun nor the unexampled slaughter could for a moment restrain. At six o'clock, when the king sent off this second courier, the enemy had retreated behind his last intrenchments, and taken refuge at Gudenberg. [Footnote: Frederick the Great.—Thiebault]

A loud hurrah broke from the people as Herzberg finished and left the balcony. Now there was no room for doubt. The enemy was overwhelmed and had fled to his last intrenchment. Would the king leave him unmolested, and would he not still drive the hated enemy further?

While groups of men were assembled here and there, discussing these weighty questions, and others, intoxicated, drunk with joy at this great victory over their hereditary enemy, were making eloquent addresses to the people, a third courier appeared in sight.

Breathless with expectation and anxiety, they would not give him time to reach the castle. They must—they would know the news he brings. There should be no delay, no temporizing, no mysteries. The people were one great family. They awaited the message of their father. They demanded news of their distant sons and brothers.

The third courier brings renewed assurances. The Russians are routed. The king will give them no rest. He will drive them from their last stronghold. With his whole army, with cavalry and militia, with all his cannon, he was in the act of storming Gudenberg. This is the message of the third courier.

The people are proud and happy. No one thinks of going home. In fact, they have no home but the streets. Every house would be too small for this great family which feels a thirst to express its joy and its rapture to each other. And then it was possible the king might send another courier. Who could go home till they knew that the Russians were driven from their last stronghold, that Gudenberg was drenched in Russian blood?

No one doubted that this news would come—must come. Not the slightest fear, the least doubt troubled the proud, pure joy of this hour. The victory was achieved, but it was still charming to hear it confirmed; to receive these heavenly messages. Every open space was filled with men. Each one would see and hear for himself. No man thought himself too distinguished, too sick, too weak, to stand for hours in the burning sun, carried about involuntarily by this fluctuating wave of humanity. Side by side with the laborer stood the elegant lady in her silk robes; near the poor beggar in his ragged jacket were seen the high official and the wealthy banker in their rich dresses.

Move than fifty thousand men were now assembled and waiting— waiting for what they knew not—for news—for a courier who could give the details. It was not enough to know that the king had conquered; they wished to know the extent and the significance of this victory; and lastly, they would know the bloody offering which this victory had cost. The dinner-hour was passed. What cared this happy people for dinner? They hungered for no earthly food; they thirsted for no earthly drink; they were satisfied with the joy of victory. The clock struck three. Yes, there comes a horseman, his bridle is hanging loose—he is covered with dust—but how, what means this? His face is pale as death; his eyes are misty; he looks around shame-faced and confused. No happy news is written upon this dark and clouded brow. What means this messenger of death in the midst of joy, triumph, and proud consciousness of victory? They seek to hold him, to question him, but he gives no answer. He spurs his wearied horse till he springs aloft, and the men in rash terror are crushed against each other; but the horseman makes no sign. Silently he dashes on through the laughing, chatting crowd, but wherever he passes, laughter and smiles disappear, and speech is silenced.

It seemed as if the angel of death had touched his brow, and the happy ones shuddered at his untimely presence. Now he has reached the castle, he descends from his horse. In breathless silence, pallid, trembling they know not why, those who have seen this dumb messenger look up shudderingly to the balcony. At last, after long waiting, the Minister Herzberg appeared once more.

But, O God! what means this? he is pale—his eyes are filled with tears. He opens his mouth to speak, but strength has left him. He holds on to the bars of the balcony, otherwise he would sink. At last he collects himself. It is not necessary to ask for silence; the silence of the grave is upon those torpid men. He speaks! his voice is faint and weak, and trembles—oh, so fearfully! only a few in the first rank can hear his words.

"The battle is lost! The Russians have conquered! The Austrians came to their assistance! The presence of the Austrians was not known, they had their tents in holes in the ground! As our militia rushed upon the last intrenchment at Judenberg and were only a hundred steps distant, Loudon suddenly advanced with his fresh troops, against the worn-out and exhausted victors. He received the Prussians with so murderous a fire, that their ranks faltered, wavered, and, at last, broke loose in wild flight, pursued furiously by the raging enemy. The fortunes of the day had turned; we lost the battle. But all is not lost. The king lives! he is slightly wounded; three horses were shot under him. He lives, and so long as he lives, there is hope. In the far distance, in the midst of the terrible disaster? which have befallen himself and his army, he thinks of his Berliners. He sends you a father's greeting, and exhorts every one of you to save his possessions, as far as possible. Those who do not feel safe in Berlin, and who fear the approaching enemy, the king counsels to withdraw, if possible, with their money, to Magdeburg, where the royal family will take refuge this evening."

The minister was silent, and the people who had listened, dumb with horror, now broke out in wild cries of anguish and despair. Terror was written in every face; tears gushed from every eye. Cries of unspeakable agony burst from those lips, which, a few moments before, were eloquent with hope and gladness.

As if it were impossible to believe in these misfortunes without further confirmation, some men called loudly for the messenger, and the distant crowd, as if inspired with new hope, roared louder and louder:

"The courier! the courier! we will ourselves speak with the courier!"

The demand was so threatening, so continuous, it must be complied with. Herzberg stepped upon the balcony, and informed the crowd that the courier would at once descend to the public square. A breathless silence succeeded; every eye was fixed upon the castle-gate, through which the courier must come. When he appeared, the crowd rushed forward toward him in mad haste. Cries of woe and suffering were heard. The people, with—mad with pain, beside themselves with despair, had no longer any mercy, any pity for each other. They rushed upon the messenger of misfortune, without regarding those who, in the midst of this wild tumult, were cast down, and trodden under foot.

The messenger began his sad story. He repeated all that the minister had said; he told of the deadly strife, of the bloody havoc, of the raging advance of the Austrians, and of the roar for vengeance of the reassured Russians. He told how the cannon-balls of the enemy had stricken down whole ranks of Prussians; that more than twenty thousand dead and wounded Prussians lay upon the battle-field; that all the cannon and all the colors had fallen into the hands of the enemy.

The people received this news with tears, cries, and lamentations. The courier spoke also of the king. He, himself, had belonged to the body-guard of the king—had been ever near him. He had seen the king standing in the midst of the thickest shower of balls, when his two adjutants fell at his side. At last, a ball came and wounded the king's horse—the Vogel—so fearfully, that the brave steed fell. Frederick mounted another horse, but remained upon the same spot; a second ball wounded this horse, and the king quietly mounted that of Captain Gotzen. At this moment, a bullet struck the king in the breast, but the golden etui which the king carried in his pocket, had turned it aside, and thus saved his life. In vain had the generals and adjutants entreated him to leave this place, and think of his personal safety. His answer was—"We must seek, at this point, to win the battle. I must do my duty here with the rest." [Footnote: The king's own words.—See Thiebaul, p. 214.]

Many voices cried out—"Where is the king now?"

The courier did not answer; but the question was so fiercely, so stormily repeated, that he was compelled to go on.

"The king, in the midst of the confusion and horror of the flight, had called him, and commanded him to gallop to Berlin, and bear the fatal news to Minister Herzberg. He had then galloped by him, exactly against the enemy, as if he wished their balls to strike him; a little troop of his most faithful soldiers had followed!"

"The king is lost! the king is a prisoner—wounded—perhaps dead!" cried the terrified people.

Suddenly, the mad tumult was interrupted by loud shouts of joy, which swelled and thundered like an avalanche from the other side of the square. A fifth courier had arrived, and brought the news of the complete defeat of the Russians, and a glorious Prussian victory. Now, one of those memorable, wondrous—grand scenes took place, which no earthly phantasy could contrive or prepare, to which only Providence could give form and color. As if driven by the storm-winds of every powerful earthly passion, this great sea of people fluctuated here and there. At one point, thousands were weeping over the news which the unhappy messenger had brought. Near by, thousands were huzzaing and shouting over the joyful intelligence brought by the fifth courier, while those who had been near enough to the fourth courier to understand his words, turned aside to give the sad news to those who were afar off. Coming at the same time from the other side, they were met by a mighty mass of men, who announced, with glad cries, the news of victory, brought by the fifth courier. Here you could see men, with their arms raised to heaven, thanking God for the hardly-won victory. A little farther on, pale, frightened creatures, motionless, bowed down, and grief-stricken. Here were women, with glowing cheeks and sparkling eyes, shouting over their hero king. There, the people wept and moaned; their king had disappeared, was a prisoner, or dead. As at the Tower of Babel, the people spoke in a thousand tongues, and no one listened to another; every one was lost—blinded by his own passionate hopes and fears.

At last the two couriers were called upon to come face to face and decide these important questions. Strong men lifted them upon their shoulders and brought them together; a profound and fearful silence ensued, every man felt that he stood upon the eve of a mighty revelation; fifty thousand men were waiting breathlessly for news of happiness beyond compare, or of unspeakable woe. The conversation of the two horsemen standing upon the shoulders of their townsmen was quick and laconic.

"At what hour did the king send you off?" said the fourth courier to the fifth.

"At six. The king himself commissioned me."

"Where stood our army at that time?" said the fourth courier.

"They stood before the hollow ground, and the Russians had withdrawn to the intrenchments of Zudenberg; we had taken a hundred and twenty cannon, and many of our soldiers were wandering about the battle-field looking at the batteries they had taken." [Footnote: Bodman.]

"Yes," said the fourth courier, sadly, "that was at six, but at seven we were in full flight. Loudon had risen from the ground, and the frightened, conquered Russians had recovered themselves. You left at six, I at eight; I have ridden more rapidly than you. Unhappily, I am right, the battle is lost!"

"The battle is lost!" howled the people; "the king is also lost! Woe! woe!"

At this moment the royal equipages were seen making their way slowly through the crowd, and the advance guard were praying the people to open a way for the travelling carriages to reach the castle. These words excited new alarm. "We are lost! Let us fly, let us fly! The court, the queen, and the princesses flee—let us save ourselves! The Russians will come to Berlin— they will annihilate us. We are deserted and lost, lost!—no one knows where our king is!"

As if driven by madness, the crowds rushed against each other, like the sea when it divides, and in billowy streams pours itself out here and there; and the cry of anguish which now rang out from the castle square, found its echo in every street and every house.

CHAPTER XI
AFTER THE BATTLE

The cannon were silenced, the discharges of musketry had ceased. On the great plain of Kunersdorf, where, a few hours before, a bloody battle had been raging, all was quiet. Could this be called repose? How cruel was the tranquillity which rested now upon this fearful battle-field!

It was the peace of death—the stillness which the awful messenger of Heaven presses as a sign and seal of his love upon the pale lips of the dead. Happy they whose immortal spirits were quickly wafted away by the dread kiss—they no longer suffer. Woe to those who yet live, though they belong to death, and who lie surrounded by grinning corpses! The cold bodies of their comrades are the pillows upon which they lay their bloody heads. The groans of the dying form the awful melody which awakes them to consciousness; and the, starry sky of this clear, transparent summer night is the only eye of love which bows down to them and looks upon them in their agony.

Happy those whom the murderous sword and the crushing ball carried off in an instant to the land of spirits! Woe, woe to those lying upon the battle-field, living, breathing, conscious of their defeat and of their great agony! Woe! woe! for they hear the sound of the tramping and neighing of horses—they come nearer and nearer. The moon throws the long, dark shadows of those advancing horse-men over the battle-field. It is fearful to see their rash approach; spurring over thousands of pale corpses, not regarding the dying, who breathe out their last piteous sighs under the hoofs of these wild horses.

The Cossack has no pity; he does not shudder or draw back from this monstrous open grave, which has received thousands of men as if they were one great corpse. The Cossack has come to rob and to plunder; he spares neither friend nor foe. He is the heir of the dead and of the dying, and he has come for his inheritance. If he sees a ring sparkling upon the hand of a grinning corpse, he springs from his horse and tears it off. If his greedy, cruel eye rests upon a rich uniform he seizes it, he tears it off from the bleeding, wounded body, no matter whether it is dead or still breathing and rattling.

Look at that warrior who, groaning with anguish, his limbs torn to pieces, bleeding from a thousand wounds, is lying in an open grave; he is wounded to death; he still holds his sword in his left hand—his right arm has been torn off by a cannon-ball, a shot that he might not be trampled upon by the horses' hoofs; they are forced to leave him in the hands of God and to the mercy of man.

But the Cossack knows no mercy. That is a word he has never heard in his Russian home; he has no fear of God before his eyes—he fears the Czar and his captain, and above all other things, he fears the knout. He knows nothing of pity, for it has never been shown him—how then should he exercise it?

When the Cossack saw the Prussian officer in his gold-embroidered uniform, he sprang from his horse and threw the bridle over him, a shrill whistle told the wild steed, the Cossack's better half, that he must stand still. He sprang into the grave where the Prussian warrior, the German poet, was laid to rest. Yes, a great German poet lies there—a poet by the grace of God. All Germany knows him, "their songster of the spring." All Germany had read and been inspired by his lays. The Austrian and the Saxon considered the Prussian Major Ewald von Kleist their enemy, but they loved and admired the poet, Ewald von Kleist. The people are never enemies to poesy, and even politics are silent before her melodious voice.

There he lies, the gallant warrior, the inspired, noble poet; his broken eyes are turned to heaven; his blue, cold lips are opened and wearily stammering a few disconnected words. Perhaps he thinks in this last hour of the last words of his last poem. Perhaps his stiffening lips murmured these words which his mangled hand had written just before the battle:

> *"Death for one's fatherland is ever honorable.*
>
> *How gladly will I die that noble death*
>
> *When my destiny calls!"*

Yes, death might have been beautiful, but fate is never propitious to German poets. It would have been noble and sweet to die in the wild tumult of battle, under the sound of trumpets, amid the shouts of victory; sweet thus, with a smile upon the lip to yield up the immortal spirit.

Ewald von Kleist, the German poet, received his death-wound upon the field of battle, but he did not die there; he lives, he knows that the battle is lost, that his blood has been shed in vain. The Cossack has come down into his grave—with greedy eyes he gazes at the rich booty. This bleeding, mangled body—this is to the Cossack not a man, it is only a uniform which is his; with hands trembling with greed he tears it from the quivering, bleeding form. What to him is the death-rattle and the blood—even the bloody shirt dying frame. *[Footnote: "History of the Seven Years' War."—Thiebault, 363.]* The Prussian warrior, the German poet, lay there naked, his own blood alone covered his wounded body, wrapped it in a purple mantle, worthy of the poet's crown with which his countrymen had decked his brow.

But Ewald von Kleist is no longer a poet or a hero—he is a poor, suffering, tortured child of earth; he lies on the damp ground, he pleads for a few rags to cover his wounds, into which the muddy water of the hole in which he lies is rushing.

And now fate seems favorable. A Russian officer is riding by—he takes pity on the naked man with the gaping wounds; he throws him a soldier's old mantle, a piece of bread, and a half gulden. *[Footnote: "Seven Years' War," 353.]* The German poet receives the alms of the Russian thankfully—he covers himself with the cloak, he tries to eat the bread.

But destiny is never propitious to German poets. The Cossacks swarm again upon the battle-field, and again they approach the groaning warrior in the open grave; he has no longer a glittering uniform, but the Cossack takes all; the poor old mantle excites his greed—he tears it from the unresisting soldier; he opens his hands and takes out the half gulden which Ewald von Kleist had received from the Russian hussar.

Again he lies naked, again the muddy water forces into his wounds, and adds cruel torture to the agonies of death. So lies he till the next day, till the enemy takes pity upon him and carries him as a prisoner to Frankfort. *[Footnote: Ewald von Kleist died a few days after this, on the 24th of August. The Russians gave him an honorable burial; and as there was no sword upon his coffin, Captain Bulow, chief of the Russian dragoons, took his own from his side and placed it upon the bier, saying, "So worthy an officer shall not be buried without every mark of honor."—Archenholtz, 262.]*

Happy those who meet with sudden death. It is true all the living did not share the cruel fate of Ewald von Kleist, but all those thousands who were borne wounded and bleeding from the battle-field were conscious of their sufferings and their defeat.

The little village of Octshef near the battle-field was a hospital. During the battle all the inhabitants had fled. The wounded had taken possession of the huts and the surgeons were hastening from house to house giving relief where it was possible. No one entered into those two little huts which lay at the other end of the village, somewhat separated from the others. And yet those huts contained two wounded men. They had been brought here during the battle—the surgeon had examined their wounds and gone out silently, never to return. Groaning from time to time, these two wounded men lay upon the straw, their eyes fixed upon the door, longing for the surgeon to bring them help, or at least alleviation.

And now the door was indeed opened, and an officer entered. Was it the obscurity of twilight, or had blood and pain blinded the eyes of the wounded men so that, they could not recognize the stranger? It was true his noble and generally cheerful face was now grave and stern, his cheeks were ashy pale, and his great, flashing eyes were dim; but there was still something inexpressibly majestic and commanding in his appearance—though defeated and cast down, he was still a hero, a king—Frederick the Great!

Frederick had come to take up his quarters in this lonely hut, to be alone in his great grief; but when he saw the two wounded men, his expression changed to one of earnest sympathy. With hasty steps he drew near to the two officers, bowed over and questioned them kindly. They recognized his voice—that voice which had so often inspired them to bold deeds in the wild whirl of battle, but whose tones were now mild and sympathetic.

"The king!" cried both in joyful surprise, and forgetting their wounds and helplessness, they strove to rise, but sank back with hollow groans, with the blood streaming anew from their wounds.

"Poor children," said Frederick, "you are badly wounded."

"Yes," groaned Lieutenant von Grabow, "badly wounded, but that is of small consequence, if, your majesty, we only knew that we had gained the day. We had taken two redoubts, and were storming the third, when this misfortune befell us. Tell us, your majesty, is it not true? Is not the victory ours?"

A dark shadow passed over the face of the king, but soon disappeared.

"You must now think only of yourselves. You have proved that you are brave—the rest is accident or fate. Do not despond, all will be well. Have your wounds been dressed? Have you been fed?"

"Ah, sire, no devil will dress our wounds," groaned Lieutenant von Hubenfall.

"How," cried the king, "have they left you here without care and assistance?"

"Yes, sire, there is no earthly hope for us."

The king was about to answer, when several people, bearing hand-barrows, accompanied by a surgeon, entered.

"What do you wish?" said the king, angrily.

"Sire," answered the surgeon, "we will remove the wounded, as your majesty will make your night-quarters here."

The king threw a scornful glance upon them.

"And you suppose that I will allow this? The wounded men remain here. I will seek shelter elsewhere. But, above all things, examine the wounds of these two officers at once, and dress them."

The surgeon advanced, and examined them carefully, then drew near the king.

"Your majesty," said he, shrugging his shoulders, "it would be all in vain. A cannon-ball has torn off the right arm of one of these men, and he must die of gangrene. The other has a cartridge-load of iron in his face and in his body. It is impossible to bind up these wounds."

The king did not answer him. He stepped hastily to the straw-bed, and took both the wounded men by the hand. Then, turning to the surgeon, he said—

"Look, now, these two men are young and powerful—they have no fever. With such young blood and fresh hearts Nature often does wonders. Dress them, and bind up their wounds, and, above all things, see that they have nourishment—they have need of it."

"Ah, yes, your majesty; we have been hungry and thirsty a long time," said Grabow.

The king smiled. "See, now, you think they are lost, and yet they have healthy stomachs; so long as a man is hungry he will not die."

The surgeon opened his case of instruments and commenced to dress the wounds. The king watched him for a long time, then stooped down and said, tenderly, "Children, do not despair; I will learn how it goes with you, and if you are no longer fit for service, I will take care of you. Believe that I will not forget you." He bowed kindly and left the room. His adjutants were awaiting him at the door of the tent. [*Footnote: The king's own words. The whole scene is historical. These two officers, whom the king saved in this way from death, recovered rapidly. After they were completely restored, they again took part in the contest, and were again severely wounded at Kolberg. They served until peace was declared, and then retired on the invalid list, and, by the express order of the king, were most kindly cared for.—See Nicolai.*] The king signed to them to follow him, and stepping rapidly through the village, he passed by the huts from which loud cries of anguish and low murmurs were heard.

"Ah," cried Frederick, "Dante did not know all the horrors of hell, or he forgot to paint those I now suffer." He hastened on—on—on, in the obscure twilight of the summer night, pursued by the sighs and groans of his dying and wounded soldiers; a deep, immeasurable sadness lay upon his brow; his lips were trembling; cold perspiration stood upon his forehead; his eyes wandered over the battle-field, then were raised to heaven with a questioning and reproachful expression. Already the village lay far behind him; but he hurried on, he had no aim, no object; he wished only to escape this hell, this cry of despair and woe from the condemned. An adjutant dared at last to step forward and awake him from his sad mood.

"Sire," said he, "the Cossacks are swarming in every direction, and if your majesty goes on, the most fearful results may be anticipated. The Cossacks shoot at every man who wears a good coat."

The king shook his head sadly. "There is no ball for me," said he in a low tone; "I have in vain called upon death. I have prayed in mercy for a ball; it came, but it only grazed my breast. No, no—there is no ball for me!" He advanced, and the adjutant dared once more to interrupt him.

"Sire," said he, "will not your majesty seek night-quarters?"

Frederick raised his head, and was in the act of answering hastily, then said: "Yes, I need night-quarters." He looked around and saw an empty peasant's house by the wayside, drew near and entered silently.

CHAPTER XII
A HEROIC SOUL

"I will pass the night here," said he, "the place appears deserted; we will disturb no one."

The king was right. The miserable old hut was empty. No one advanced to meet him as he entered. In one corner of the room there was some dirty straw; in the other a wooden table and stool—this was all.

"It suffices for me," said the king, smiling. "I will pass the night here. Have you my writing materials with you?"

"I sent Adjutant von Goltz for them, sire, as I did not wish to leave you alone."

Goltz now entered with the king's portfolio, and informed him that he had brought two grenadiers to guard the house.

"Have I still grenadiers?" murmured the king, in a trembling voice. His head fell upon his breast, and he stood thus lost in deep thought for a while. "Gentlemen," said he, at length, "inspect the house. See if there is a more comfortable room than this; if not, I suppose we can manage to sleep here. Send one of the guard for some soldiers, by whom I can forward my dispatches."

The adjutants bowed, and left the room. The king was alone. He could at last give way to his despair—his grief.

"All, all is lost!" murmured the king, and a voice within him answered: "When all is lost, there is no escape but death! It is unworthy to continue a life without fame, without glory. The grave alone is a resting-place for the broken-hearted, humiliated man!"

The king listened attentively to this voice. He had borne with patience the sorrows and deprivations of the past years, but he could not survive the ruin of his country. His country was lost. There was no chance of saving it; his army was gone. The victorious enemy had taken all the neighboring provinces. The Russians could now march undisturbed to Berlin. They would find no resistance, for the garrison there consisted of invalids and cripples.

Berlin was lost! Prussia was lost! The king was resolved to die, for he was a king without a crown, a hero without laurels. He wished to die, for he could not survive the destruction of his country. But first he must arrange his affairs, make his will, and bid adieu to his friends. The king opened the door hastily, and desired that a light should be brought—it was no easy thing to procure in this dismal, deserted village. The adjutant succeeded at last, however, in getting a few small tallow candles, and placing them in old bottles, in the absence of candlesticks of any description, he carried them to the king. Frederick did not observe him; he stood at the open window, gazing earnestly at the starry firmament. The bright light aroused him; he turned, and approached the table.

"My last letters!" murmured he, sinking upon the wooden stool, and opening his portfolio.

How his enemies would have rejoiced, could they have seen him in that wretched hovel! He first wrote to General Fink, to whom he wished to leave the command of his army. He must fulfil the duties of state, before those of friendship. It was not a letter—rather an order to General Fink, and read as follows:

"General Fink will find this a weary and tedious commission. The army I leave is no longer in a condition to defend itself from the Russians. Haddeck will hasten to Berlin. Loudon also, I presume. If you intercept them, the Russians will be in your rear; if you remain by the Oder, Haddeck will surround you. I nevertheless believe, were Loudon to come to Berlin, you could attack and defeat him. This, were it possible, would give you time to arrange matters, and I can assure you, time is every thing, in such desperate circumstances as ours. Koper, my secretary, will give you the dispatches from Torgau and Dresden. You must acquaint my brother, whom I make general-in-chief of the army, with all that passes. In the mean time, his orders must be obeyed. The army must swear by my nephew. This is the only advice I am able to give. Had I any resources, I would stand fast by you. FREDERICK." [Footnote: The king's own words.]

"Yes, I would have stood by them," murmured the king, as he folded and addressed his letter. "I would have borne still longer this life of oppression and privation; but now, honor demands that I should die."

He took another sheet of paper. It was now no order or command, but a tender, loving, farewell letter to his friend, General Finkenstein.

"This morning, at eleven o'clock, I attacked the enemy; we drove them back to Gudenberg. All my men performed deeds of daring and bravery, but, at the storming of Gudenberg, a terrific number of lives were lost. My army became separated. I reassembled them three times, but in vain. At last, they fled in wild disorder. I very nearly became a prisoner, and was obliged to leave the field to the enemy. My uniform was torn by the cannon-balls, two horses were shot underneath me, but death shunned me; I seemed to bear a charmed life; I could not die! From an army of forty-eight thousand men, there now remains three thousand. The consequences of this battle will be more fearful than the battle itself. It is a terrible misfortune, and I will not survive it. There is no one to whom I can look for help. I cannot survive my country's ruin. Farewell!"

"And now," said the king, when he had sealed and directed his letter, "now I am ready; my worldly affairs are settled. I am at the end of my sufferings, and dare claim that last, deep rest granted by Nature to us all. I have worked enough, suffered enough; and if, after a life of stormy disasters, I seek my grave, no one can say it was cowardly not to live—for all the weight of life rolled upon me, forced me to the ground, and the grave opened beneath my feet. I continued to hope, when overwhelmed with defeat at every point. Every morning brought new clouds, new sorrows. I bore it courageously, trusting that misfortune would soon weary, the storms blow over, and a clear, cloudless sky envelop me. I deceived myself greatly; my sorrows increased. And now, the worst has happened; my country is lost! Who dares say I should survive this loss? To die at the proper time is also a duty. The Romans felt this, and acted upon it. I am a true scholar of the old masters, and wish to prove myself worthy of them. When all is lost, the liberty to die should not be denied. The world has nothing more to do with me, and I laugh at her weak, unjust laws. Like Tiberius, will I live and die! Farewell, then, thou false existence; farewell, weak man! Ah! there are so many fools—so few men amongst you; I have found so many faithless friends, so many traitors, so few honest men! In the hour of misfortune they all deserted me! But, no!" said he; "one remained true. D'Argens never deceived me, and I had almost forgotten to take leave of him. Well, death must wait for me, while I write to D'Argens!"

A heavenly inspiration now beamed on his countenance; his eyes shone like stars. The holy muse had descended to comfort the despairing hero, to whisper loving and precious words to him. Thus standing at death's portals, Frederick wrote his most beautiful poem, called "Ami le sort en est jete'." A great wail of woe burst from his soul. The sorrows, the grievances hid until now from all, he portrayed in touching, beautiful words to his absent friend. He pictured to him his sufferings, his hopes, his struggles, and finally, his determination to die. When all this had been painted in the most glowing colors, when his wounds were laid bare, he wrote a last and touching farewell to his friend:

"Adieu, D'Argens! dans ce tableau,

De mon trepas tu vois la cause;

Au moins ne pense pas du neant du caveau,

Que j'aspire a l'apotheose.

Tout ce que l'amitie par ces vers propose,

C'est que tant qu'ici-bas le celeste flambeau;

Eclairera tes jours tandis que je repose,

Et lorsque le printemps paraissant de nouveau.

De son sein abondant t'offre les fleurs ecloses,

Chaque fois d'un bouquet de myrthes et de roses,

Tu daignes parer mon tombeau."

[Footnote:

"Adieu, D'Argens! In this picture

Thou wilt see the cause of my death;

At least, do not think, a nothing in the vault,

That I aspire to apotheosis.

All that friendship by these lines proposes

Is only this much, that here the celestial torch

May clear thy days while I repose,

And each time when the Spring appears anew

And from her abundant breast offers thee the flowers there enclosed

That thou with a bouquet of myrtle and rose

Wilt deign to decorate my tomb."]

"Ah!" murmured the king, as he folded and addressed his poetical letter, "how lovely it must now be at Sans-Souci! Well, well! my grave shall be there, and D'Argens will cover it with flowers. And have I no other friends at Sans-Souci? My good old hounds, my crippled soldiers! They cannot come to me, but I will go to them."

The king then arose, opened the door, and asked if a messenger was in readiness; receiving an answer in the affirmative, he gave the three letters to the adjutant. "And now my work is finished," said he, "now I can die." He took from his breast-pocket a small casket of gold which he always carried with him, and which, in the late battle, had served him as a shield against the enemy's balls. The lid had been hollowed in by a ball; strange to say, this casket, which had saved his life, was now to cause his death. For within it there was a small vial containing three pills of the most deadly poison, which the king had kept with him since the beginning of the war. The king looked at the casket thoughtfully. "Death here fought against death; and still how glorious it would have been to die upon the battle-field believing myself the victor!" He held the vial up to the light and shook it; and as the pills bounded up and down, he said, smiling sadly, "Death is merry! It comes eagerly to invite me to the dance. Well, well, my gay cavalier, I am ready for the dance."

He opened the vial and emptied the pills into his hand. Then arose and approached the window to see once more the sky with its glittering stars and its brightly-beaming moon, and the battle-field upon which thousands of his subjects had this day found their death. Then raised the hand with the pills. What was it that caused him to hesitate? Why did his hand fall slowly down? What were his eyes so intently gazing on?

The king was not gazing at the sky, the stars, or the moon; but far off into the distance, at the Austrian camp-fires. There were the conquerors, there was Soltikow and Loudon with their armies. The king had observed these fires before entering the hut, but their number had now increased, a sign that the enemy had not advanced, but was resting. How? Was it possible that the enemy, not taking advantage of their victory, was not following the conquered troops, but giving them time to rally, to outmarch them, perhaps time to reach the Spree, perhaps Berlin?

"If this is so," said the king, answering his own thoughts, "if the enemy neglects to give me the finishing-blow, all is not lost. If there is a chance of salvation for my country, I must not die; she needs me, and it is, my duty to do all in my power to retrieve the past."

He looked again at the camp-fires, and a bright smile played about his lips.

"If those fires speak aright," said he, "my enemies are more generous—or more stupid—than I thought, and many advantages may still be derived from this lost battle. If so, I must return to my old motto that 'life is a duty.' And so long as good, honorable work is to be done, man has no right to seek the lazy rest of the grave. I must ascertain at once if my suspicions are correct. Death may wait awhile. As long as there is a necessity for living, I cannot die."

He returned the pills to the vial and hid the casket in its former resting-place. Then passing hastily through the room, he opened the door. The two adjutants were sitting upon the wooden bench in front of the hut; both were asleep. The grenadiers were pacing with even tread up and down before the house; deep quiet prevailed. The king stood at the door looking in amazement at the glorious scene before him. He inhaled with delight the soft summer air; never had it seemed to him so balmy, so full of strengthening power, and he acknowledged that never had the stars, the moon, the sky looked as beautiful. With lively joy he felt the night-wind toying with his hair. The king would not tire of all this; it seemed to him as if a friend, dead long since, mourned and bewailed, had suddenly appeared to him beaming with health, and as if he must open his arms and say, "Welcome, thou returned one. Fate separated us; but now, as we have met, we will never leave one another, but cling together through life and death, through good and evil report."

Life was the friend that appeared to Frederick, and he now felt his great love for it. Raising his eyes in a sort of ecstasy to the sky, he murmured, "I swear not to seek death unless at the last extremity, if, when made a prisoner, I cannot escape. I swear to live, to suffer, so long as I am free."

He had assumed the harness of life, and was determined to battle bravely with it.

CHAPTER XIII
THE TWO GRENADIERS

Smiling, and with elastic step, the king advanced to meet the two grenadiers, who stood rooted to the spot as he approached them. "Grenadiers," said he, "why are you not with your comrades?"

"Our comrades fled," said one.

"It is dishonorable to fly," said the other.

The king was startled. These voices were familiar, he had surely heard them before.

"I ought to know you," said he, "this is not the first time we have spoken together. What is your name, my son?"

"Fritz Kober is my name," said the grenadier.

"And yours?"

"Charles Henry Buschman," said the other.

"You are not mistaken, sir king! we have met and spoken before, but it was on a better night than this."

"Where was it?" said the king.

"The night before the great, the glorious battle of Leuthen," said Fritz Kober, gravely; "at that time, sir king, you sat at our tent-fire and ate dumplings with us. Charles Henry knows how to cook them so beautifully!"

"Ah! I remember," said the king; "you made me pay my share of the costs."

"And you did so, like a true king," said Fritz Kober. "Afterward you came back to our tent-fire, and Charles Henry Buschman told you fairy tales, nobody can do that so beautifully as Charles Henry, and you slept refreshingly throughout."

"No, no, grenadier," said the king, "I did not sleep, and I can tell you to-day all that Charles Henry related."

"Well, what was it?" said Fritz Kober, with great delight.

The king reflected a moment, and then said, in a soft voice:

"He told of a king who was so fondly loved by a beautiful fairy, that she changed herself into a sword when the king went to war and helped him to defeat his enemies! Is that it. Fritz Kober?"

"Nearly so, sir king; I wish you had such a fairy at your side to-day."

"Still, Fritz," whispered Charles Henry Buschman, "our king does not need the help of a fairy; our king can maintain his own cause, and God is with his sword."

"Do you truly believe that, my son?" said the king, deeply moved. "Have you still this great confidence in me? Do you still believe that I can sustain myself and that God is with me?"

"We have this confidence, and we will never lose it!" cried Charles Henry, quickly. "Our enemies over there have no Frederick to lead them on, no commander-in-chief to share with them hunger and thirst, and danger and fatigue; therefore they cannot love their leaders as we do ours."

"And then," said Fritz Kober, thoughtfully, "I am always thinking that this war is like a battle of the cats and hounds. Sometimes it looks as if the little cats would get the better of the great bulldogs; they have sharp claws, and scratch the dogs in the face till they can neither see nor hear, and must for a while give way; they go off, however, give themselves a good shake, and open their eyes, and spring forward as great and strong and full of courage as ever; they seize upon the poor cats in the nape of the neck and bite them deadly with their strong, powerful teeth. What care they if the cats do scratch in the mean while? No, no, sir king, the cats cannot hold out to the end; claws are neither so strong nor so lasting as teeth."

"Yes," said the king, laughing, "but how do you know but our foes over there are the hounds and we are the little cats?"

"What!" cried Fritz Kober, amazed, "we shall be the cats? No, no, sir king, we are the great hounds."

"But how can you prove this?"

"How shall I prove it?" said Fritz Kober, somewhat embarrassed. After a short pause, he cried out, gayly, "I have it—I will prove it. Those over there are the cats because they are Russians and Austrians, and do not serve a king as we do; they have only two empresses, two women. Now, sir king, am I not right? Women and cats, are they not alike? So those over there are the cats and we are the bull dogs!"

Frederick was highly amused. "Take care," said he, "that 'those over there' do not hear you liken their empresses to cats."

"And if they are empresses," said Fritz Kober, dryly, "they are still women, and women are cats."

The king looked over toward the camp-fires, which were boldly shining on the horizon.

"How far is it from here to those fires?" said he.

"About an hour," said Charles Henry, "not more."

"One hour," repeated the king, softly. "In one hour, then, I could know my fate! Listen, children, which of you will go for me?"

Both exclaimed in the same moment, "I will!"

"It is a fearful attempt," said the king, earnestly; "the Cossacks are swarming in every direction, and if you escape them, you may be caught in the camp and shot as spies."

"I will take care that they shall not recognize me as an enemy," said Charles Henry, quietly.

"I also," said Fritz Kober, zealously. "You stay, Charles Henry, we dare not both leave the king. You know that only this evening, while upon the watch, we swore that, even if the whole army of the enemy marched against us, we would not desert our king, but would stand at our post as long as there was a drop of blood in our veins or a breath in our bodies."

The king laid his hands upon the two soldiers and looked at them with much emotion. The moon, which stood great and full in the heavens, lighted up this curious group, and threw three long, dark shadows over the plain.

"And you have sworn that, my children?" said the king, after a long pause. "Ah, if all my men thought as you do we would not have been defeated this day."

"Sir king, your soldiers all think as we do, but fate was against us. Just as I said, the cats outnumbered us to-day, but we will bite them bravely for it next time. And now tell me, sir king, what shall I do over there in the camp?"

Before the king could answer, Charles Henry laid his hand upon his arm.

"Let me go," said he, entreatingly; "Fritz Kober is so daring, so undaunted, he is not cautious; they will certainly shoot him, and then you have lost the best soldier in your army."

"Your loss, I suppose, would not be felt; the king can do without you."

"Listen, children," said the king, "it is best that you both go; one can protect the other, and four ears are better than two."

"The king is right, that is best—we will both go."

"And leave the king alone and unguarded?"

"No," said the king, pointing to the two sleepers, "I have my two adjutants, and they will keep guard for me. Now, listen to what I have to say to you. Over there is the enemy, and it is most important for me to know what he is doing, and what he proposes to do. Go, then, and listen. Their generals have certainly taken up their quarters in the village. You must ascertain that positively, and then draw near their quarters. You will return as quickly as possible, and inform me of all that you hear and see."

"Is that all?" said Fritz Kober.

"That is all. Now be off, and if you do your duty well, and return fresh and in good order, you shall be both made officers." Fritz Kober laughed aloud. "No, no, sir king, we know that old story already."

"It is not necessary that you should promise us any thing, your majesty," said Charles Henry; "we do not go for a reward, but for respect and love to our king."

"But tell me, Fritz Kober, why you laughed so heartily?" said the king.

"Because this is not the first time that your majesty has promised to make us officers. Before the battle of Leuthen, you said if we were brave and performed valiant deeds, you would make us officers. Well, we were brave. Charles Henry took seven prisoners, and I took nine; but we are not officers."

"You shall be to-morrow," said the king. "Now, hasten off, and come back as quickly as possible."

"We will leave our muskets here," said Charles Henry; "we dare not visit our enemies in Prussian array."

They placed their arms at the house door, and then clasping each other's hands, and making a military salute, they hastened off. The king looked after them till their slender forms were lost in the distance.

"With fifty thousand such soldiers I could conquer the world," murmured he; "they are of the true metal."

He turned, and stepping up to the two sleepers, touched them lightly on the shoulders. They sprang up alarmed when they recognized the king.

"You need not excuse yourselves," said Frederick kindly, "you have had a day of great fatigue, and are, of course, exhausted. Come into the house, the night air is dangerous; we will sleep here together."

"Where are the two grenadiers?" said Goltz.

"I have sent them off on duty."

"Then your majesty must allow us to remain on guard. I have slept well, and am entirely refreshed."

"I also," said the second lieutenant. "Will your majesty be pleased to sleep? we will keep guard."

"Not so," said the king, "the moon will watch over us all. Come in."

"But it is impossible that your majesty should sleep thus, entirely unguarded. The first Cossack that dashes by could take aim at your majesty through the window."

Frederick shook his head gravely. "The ball which will strike me will come from above, [Footnote: The king's own words.—See Nicolai, p. 118.]and that you cannot intercept. No, it is better to have no watch before the door; we will not draw the attention of troops passing by to this house. I think no one will suppose that this miserable and ruinous barrack, through which the wind howls, is the residence of a king. Come, then, messieurs." He stepped into the hut, followed by the two adjutants, who dared no longer oppose him. "Put out that light," said the king, "the moon will be our torch, and will glorify our bed of straw." He drew his sword, and grasping it firmly in his right hand, he stretched himself upon the straw. "There is room for both of you—lie down. Good-night, sirs."

Frederick slightly raised his three-cornered hat in greeting, and then laid it over his face as a protection from the moonlight and the cold night air. The adjutants laid down silently at his feet, and soon no sound was heard in the room but the loud breathing of the three sleepers.

CHAPTER XIV
THE RIGHT COUNSEL

Hand in hand the two grenadiers advanced directly toward the battlefield. Before they could approach the enemy's camp they must borrow two Austrian uniforms from the dead upon the plain. It was not difficult, amongst so many dead bodies, to find two Austrian officers, and the two Prussian grenadiers went quickly to work to rob the dead and appropriate their garments.

"I don't know how it is," said Charles Henry, shuddering, "a cold chill thrills through me when I think of putting on a coat which I have just taken from a dead body. It seems to me the marble chillness of the corpse will insinuate itself into my whole body, and that I shall never be warm again."

Fritz Kober looked up with wide-open eyes! "You have such curious thoughts, Charles Henry, such as come to no other man; but you are right, it is a frosty thing." And now he had removed the uniform and was about to draw off his own jacket and assume the white coat of the Austrian. "It is a great happiness," said he, "that we need not change our trousers, a little clearer or darker gray can make no difference in the night."

Charles Henry was in the act of drawing on the coat of the dead man, when Fritz Kober suddenly seized his arm and held him back. "Stop," said he, "you must do me a favor—this coat is too narrow, and it pinches me fearfully; you are thinner than I am, and I think it will fit you exactly; take it and give me yours." He jerked off the coat and handed it to his friend.

"No, no, Fritz Kober," said Charles Henry, in a voice so soft and sweet, that Fritz was confused and bewildered by it. "No, Fritz, I understand you fully. You have the heart of an angel; you only pretend that this coat is too narrow for you that you may induce me to take the one you have already warmed."

It was well that Fritz had his back turned to the moon, otherwise his friend would have seen that his face was crimson; he blushed as if detected in some wicked act. However, he tore the uniform away from Charles Henry rather roughly, and hastened to put it on.

"Folly," said he, "the coat squeezes me, that is all! Besides, it is not wise to fool away our time in silly talking. Let us go onward."

"Directly over the battle-field?" said Charles Henry, shuddering.

"Directly over the battle-field," said Kober, "because that is the nearest way."

"Come, then," said Charles, giving him his hand.

It was indeed a fearful path through which they must walk. They passed by troops of corpses—by thousands of groaning, rattling, dying men—by many severely wounded, who cried out to them piteously for mercy and help! Often Charles Henry hesitated and stood still to offer consolation to the unhappy wretches, but Fritz Kober drew him on. "We cannot help them, and we have far to go!" Often the swarming Cossacks, dashing around on their agile little ponies, called to them from afar off in their barbarous speech, but when they drew near and saw the Austrian uniforms, they passed them quietly, and were not surprised they had not given the pass-word.

At last they passed the battle-field, and came on the open plain, at the end of which they perceived the camp-fires of the Russians and Austrians. The nearer they approached, the more lively was the scene. Shouts, laughter, loud calls, and outcries—from time to time a word of command. And in the midst of this mad confusion, here and there soldiers were running, market-women offering them wares cheap, and exulting soldiers assembling around the camp-fires. From time to time the regular step of the patrouille was heard, who surrounded the camp, and kept a watchful eye in every direction.

Arm in arm they passed steadily around the camp. "One thing I know," whispered Fritz Kober, "they have no thought of marching. They will pass a quiet, peaceful night by their camp-fires."

"I agree with you," said Charles Henry, "but let us go forward and listen a little; perhaps we can learn where the generals are quartered."

"Look, look! it must be there," said Fritz Kober, hastily.

"There are no camp-fires; but there is a brilliant light in the peasants' huts, and it appears to me that I see a guard before the doors. These, certainly, are the headquarters."

"Let us go there, then," said Charles Henry; "but we must approach the houses from behind, and thus avoid the guard."

They moved cautiously around, and drew near the houses. Profound quiet reigned in this neighborhood; it was the reverence of subordination— the effect which the presence of superior officers ever exercises upon their men. Here stood groups of officers, lightly whispering together—there soldiers were leading their masters' horses; not far off orderlies were waiting on horseback—sentinels with shouldered arms were going slowly by. The attention of all seemed to be fixed upon the two small houses, and every glance and every ear was turned eagerly toward the brilliantly lighted windows.

"We have hit the mark exactly," whispered Fritz Kober; he had succeeded with his friend in forcing his way into the little alley which separated the two houses. "We have now reached the head-quarters of the generals. Look! there is an Austrian sentinel with his bear's cap. Both the Austrian and Russian generals are here."

"Let us watch the Russians a little through the window," said Charles Henry, slipping forward.

They reached the corner, and were hidden by the trunk of a tree which overshadowed the huts. Suddenly they heard the word of command, and there was a general movement among the files of soldiers assembled about the square. The officers placed themselves in rank, the soldiers presented arms; for, at this moment, the Austrian General Loudon, surrounded by his staff, stepped from one of the small houses into the square. The Cossacks, who were crouched down on the earth before the door, raised themselves, and also presented arms.

While Loudon stood waiting, the two Prussian grenadiers slipped slyly to the other hut.

"Let us go behind," whispered Charles Henry. "There are no sentinels there, and perhaps we may find a door, and get into the house."

Behind the hut was a little garden whose thick shrubs and bushes gave complete concealment to the two grenadiers. Noiselessly they sprang over the little fence, and made a reconnoissance of the terrain—unseen, unnoticed, they drew near the house. As they stepped from behind the bushes, Fritz Kober seized his friend's arm, and with difficulty suppressed a cry of joy.

The scene which was presented to them was well calculated to rejoice the hearts of brave soldiers. They had reached the goal, and might now hope to fulfil the wishes of their king. The quarters of the Russian general were plainly exposed to them. In this great room, which was evidently the ball-room of the village, at a long oak-table, in the middle of the room, sat General Soltikow, and around him sat and stood the generals and officers. At the door, half a dozen Cossacks were crouching, staring sleepily on the ground. The room was brilliantly illuminated with wax-lights, and gave the two grenadiers an opportunity of seeing it in every part. Fate appeared to favor them in every way, and gave them an opportunity to hear as well as see. The window on the garden was opened to give entrance to the cool night air, and near it there was a thick branch of a tree in which a man could conceal himself.

"Look there," said Charles Henry, "I will hide in that tree. We will make our observations from different stand-points. Perhaps one of us may see what escapes the other. Let us attend closely, that we may tell all to our king."

No man in this room guessed that in the silent little garden four flashing eyes were observing all that passed.

At the table sat the Russian commander-in-chief, surrounded by his generals and officers. Before him lay letters, maps, and plans, at which he gazed from time to time, while he dictated an account of the battle to the officer sitting near him, Soltikow was preparing a dispatch for the Empress Elizabeth. A few steps farther off, in stiff military bearing, stood the officers who were giving in their reports, and whose statements brought a dark cloud to the brow of the victorious commander. Turning with a hasty movement of the head to the small man with the gold-embroidered uniform and the stiffly-frizzed wig, he said—

"Did you hear that, sir marquis? Ten thousand of my brave soldiers lie dead upon the battle-field, and as many more are severely wounded."

"It follows then," said the Marquis Montalembert, the French commissioner between the courts of Vienna, Petersburg, and Paris, "it follows then, that the king of Prussia has forty thousand dead and wounded, and, consequently, his little army is utterly destroyed."

"Who knows?" said Soltikow; "the king of Prussia is accustomed to sell his defeats dearly. I should not be at all surprised if he had lost fewer soldiers than we have." *[Footnote: Soltikow's own words—See Archenholtz, p 206.]* "Well, I think he has now nothing more to lose," said the marquis, laughing; "it rests with you to give the last coup de grace to this conquered and flying king, and forever prevent—"

The entrance of an officer interrupted him. The officer announced General von Loudon.

Soltikow arose, and advanced to the door to welcome the Austrian general. A proud smile was on his face as he gave his hand to Loudon; he did this with the air of a gracious superior who wished to be benevolent to his subordinate.

The quick, firm glance of Loudon seemed to read the haughty heart of his ally, and, no doubt for this reason, he scarcely touched Soltikow's hand. With erect head and proud step he advanced into the middle of the room.

"I resolved to come to your excellency," said Loudon, in a sharp, excited tone; "you have a large room, while in my hut I could scarcely find accommodation for you and your adjutants."

"You come exactly at the right hour," said Soltikow, with a haughty smile; "you see, we were about to hold a council of war, and consider what remains to be done."

A dark and scornful expression was seen in Loudon's countenance, and his eyes rested fiercely upon the smiling face of Soltikow.

"Impossible, general! you could not have held a council of war without me," said he, angrily.

"Oh, be composed, general," said Soltikow, smiling, "I would, without doubt, have informed you immediately of our conclusions."

"I suppose you could not possibly have come to any conclusion in my absence," said Loudon, the veins in whose forehead began to swell.

Soltikow bowed low, with the same unchanged and insolent smile.

"Let us not dispute about things which have not yet taken place, your excellency. The council of war had not commenced, but now that you are here, we may begin. Allow me, however, first to sign these dispatches which I have written to my gracious sovereign, announcing the victory which the Russian troops have this day achieved over the army of the King of Prussia."

"Ah, general, this time I am in advance of you," cried Loudon; "the dispatches are already sent off in which I announced to my empress the victory which the Austrian troops gained over the Prussians."

Soltikow threw his head back scornfully, and his little gray eyes flashed at the Austrian.

Loudon went on, calmly: "I assure your excellency that enthusiasm at our glorious victory has made me eloquent. I pictured to my empress the picturesque moment in which the conquering Prussians were rushing forward to take possession of the batteries deserted by the flying Russians, at which time the Austrian horsemen sprang, as it were, from the ground, checked the conquerors, and forced them back; and by deeds of lionlike courage changed the fate of the day."

While Loudon, seeming entirely cool and careless, thus spoke, the face of the Russian general was lurid with rage. Panting for breath, he pressed his doubled fist upon the table.

Every one looked at him in breathless excitement and horror—all knew his passionate and unrestrained rage. But the Marquis Montalembert hastened to prevent this outburst of passion, and before Soltikow found breath to speak, he turned with a gay and conciliating expression to Loudon.

"If you have painted the battle of to-day so much in detail," said he, "you have certainly not forgotten to depict the gallant conduct of the Russian troops to describe that truly exalted movement, when the Russians threw themselves to the earth, as if dead, before advancing columns of the Prussian army, and allowed them to pass over them; then, springing up, shot them in the back." *[Footnote: Archenholtz, Seven Years' War, p. 257.]*

"Certainly I did not forget that," said Loudon, whose noble, generous heart already repented his momentary passion and jealousy; "certainly, I am not so cowardly and so unconscionable as to deny the weighty share which the Russian army merit in the honor of this day; but you can well understand that I will not allow the gallant deeds of the Austrians to be swept away. We have fought together and conquered together, and now let us rejoice together over the glorious result."

Loudon gave his hand to Soltikow with so friendly an expression that he could not withstand it. "You are right, Loudon; we will rejoice together over this great victory," cried he. "Wine, here! We will first drink a glass in honor of the triumph of the day; then we will empty a glass of your beautiful Rhine wine to the friendship of the Austrians and Russians. Wine here! The night is long enough for council; let us first celebrate our victory."

The Cossacks, at a sign from the adjutants, sprang from the floor and drew from a corner of the room a number of bottles and silver cups, which they hastened to place upon the table. The secretaries moved the papers, maps, etc.; and the table, which a moment before had quite a business-like aspect, was now changed into an enticing buffet.

Soltikow looked on enraptured, but the marquis cast an anxious and significant look upon the Austrian general, which was answered with a slight shrug of the shoulders. Both knew that the brave General Soltikow, next to the thunder of cannon and the mad whirl of battle, loved nothing so well as the springing of corks and the odor of wine. Both knew that the general was as valiant and unconquerable a soldier as he was a valiant and unconquerable drinker—who was most apt while drinking to forget every thing else but the gladness of the moment. The marquis tried to make another weak attempt to remind him of more earnest duties.

"Look you, your excellency, your secretaries appear very melancholy. Will you not first hold a council of war? and we can then give ourselves undisturbed to joy and enjoyment."

"Why is a council of war necessary?" said Soltikow, sinking down into a chair and handing his cup to the Cossack behind him to be filled for the second time. "Away with business and scribbling! The dispatches to my empress are completed; seal them, Pietrowitch, and send the courier off immediately; every thing else can wait till morning. Come, generals, let us strike our glasses to the healths of our exalted sovereigns."

Loudon took the cup and drank a brave pledge, then when he had emptied the glass he said: "We should not be satisfied with sending our exalted sovereigns the news of the day's victory—it lies in our hands to inform them of the complete and irrevocable defeat of the enemy."

"How so?" said Soltikow, filling up his cup for the third time.

"If now, in place of enjoying this comfortable rest, and giving our enemy time to recover himself, we should follow up the Prussians and cut off the king's retreat, preventing him from taking possession of his old camp at Reutven, we would then be in a condition to crush him completely and put an end to this war."

"Ah, you mean that we should break up the camp at once," said Soltikow; "that we should not grant to our poor, exhausted soldiers a single hour of sleep, but lead them out again to battle and to death? No, no, sir general; the blood of my brave Russians is worth as much as the blood of other men, and I will not make of them a wall behind which the noble Dutchmen place themselves in comfortable security, while we offer up for them our blood and our life. I think we Russians have done enough; we do not need another victory to prove that we are brave. When I fight another such battle as I have fought to-day, with my staff in my hand and alone I must carry the news to Petersburg, for I shall have no soldiers left.*[Footnote: "Frederick the Great."—Geschow, p. 200.]* I have nothing to say against you, General Loudon. You have been a faithful ally; we have fought, bled, and conquered together, although not protected by a consecrated hat and sword like Field-Marshal Daun, who ever demands new victories from us while he himself is undecided and completely inactive."

"Your excellency seems to be somewhat embittered against Daun," said Loudon, with a smile he could not wholly suppress.

"Yes," said Soltikow, "I am embittered against this modern Fabius Cunctator, who finds it so easy to become renowned—who remains in Vienna and reaps the harvest which belongs rightly to you, General Loudon. You act, while he hesitates—you are full of energy and ever ready for the strife; Daun is dilatory, and while he is resolving whether to strike or not, the opportunity is lost."

"The empress, my exalted sovereign, has honored him with her especial confidence," said Loudon; "he must therefore merit it."

"Yes; and in Vienna they have honored you and myself with their especial distrust," said Soltikow, stormily, and swallowing a full cup of wine. "You, I know, receive rare and scanty praise; eulogies must be reserved for Daun. We are regarded with inimical and jealous eyes, and our zeal and our good-will are forever suspected."

"This is true," said Loudon, smiling; "it is difficult for us to believe in the sincere friendship of the Russians, perhaps, because we so earnestly desire it."

"Words, words!" said Soltikow, angrily. "The German has ever a secret aversion to the Russian—you look upon us as disguised tigers, ever ready to rob and devour your glorious culture and accomplishments. For this reason you gladly place a glass shade over yourselves when we are in your neighborhood, and show us your glory through a transparent wall that we may admire and envy. When you are living in peace and harmony, you avoid us sedulously; then the German finds himself entirely too educated, too refined, for the barbaric Russian. But when you quarrel and strive with each other, and cannot lay the storm, then you suddenly remember that the Russian is your neighbor and friend, that he wields a good sword, and knows how to hew with it right and left. You call lustily on him for help, and offer him your friendship—that means, just so long as hostilities endure and you have use for us. Even when you call us your friends you distrust us and suspect our good-will. Constant charges are brought against us in Vienna. Spresain languishes in chains—Austria charges him with treachery and want of zeal in the good cause; Fermor and Butterlin are also accused of great crimes—they have sought to make both their sincerity and ability suspected by the empress, and to bring them into reproach. This they have not deserved. I know, also, that they have charged me with disinclination to assist the allies—they declare that I have no ardor for the common cause. This makes bad blood, messieurs; and if it were not for the excellent wine in your beautiful Germany, I doubt if our friendship would stand upon a sure footing. Therefore, sir general, take your cup and let us drink together— drink this glorious wine to the health of our friendship. Make your glasses ring, messieurs, and that the general may see that we mean honorably with our toast, empty them at a draught."

They all accepted the challenge and emptied a cup of the old, fiery Rhine wine, which Soltikow so dearly loved; their eyes flashed, their cheeks were glowing.

Loudon saw this with horror, and he cast an anxious glance at Montalembert, who returned it with a significant shrug of the shoulder.

"And now, your excellency," said Loudon, "that we have enjoyed the German wine, let us think a little of Germany and the enemy who can no longer disturb her peace, if we act promptly. Our troops have had some hours' rest, and will now be in a condition to advance."

"Always the same old song," said Soltikow, laughing; "but I shall not be waked up from my comfortable quarters; I have done enough! my troops also."

"I have just received a courier from Daun," said Loudon, softly; "he makes it my duty to entreat your excellency to follow up our victory and crush the enemy completely."

"That will be easy work," said Montalembert, in a flattering tone. "The army of the King of Prussia is scattered and flying in every direction; they must be prevented from reassembling; the scattering troops must be harassed and more widely separated, and every possibility of retreat cut off for Frederick."

"Well, well, if that must be," said Soltikow, apathetically, placing the cup just filled with wine to his lips, "let Field-Marshal Daun undertake the duty. I have won two battles; I will wait and rest; I make no other movements till I hear of two victories won by Daun. It is not reasonable or just for the troops of my empress to act alone." *[Footnote: Soltikow's own words.—See Archenholtz, p. 266.]*

"But," said the Marquis Montalembert, giving himself the appearance of wishing not to be heard by Loudon, "if your excellency now remains inactive and does not press forward vigorously, the Austrians alone will reap the fruits of your victory."

"I am not at all disposed to be jealous," said Soltikow, laughing; "from my heart I wish the Austrians more success than I have had. For my part, I have done enough. *[Footnote: Historical.]* Fill your glasses, messieurs, fill your glasses! We have won a few hours of happiness from the goddess Bellona; let us enjoy them and forget all our cares. Let us drink once more, gentlemen. Long live our charming mistress, the Empress Elizabeth!" The Russian officers clanged their glasses and chimed in zealously, and the fragrant Rhine wine bubbled like foaming gold in the silver cups. Soltikow swallowed it with ever-increasing delight, and he became more and more animated.

The officers sat round the table with glowing cheeks and listened to their worshipped general who, in innocent gayety, related some scenes from his youth, and made his hearers laugh so loud, so rapturously, that the walls trembled, and Fritz Kober, who was crouching down in the bushes, could with difficulty prevent himself from joining in heartily.

The gayety of the Russians became more impetuous and unbridled. They dreamed of their home; here and there they began to sing Russian love-songs. The Cossacks, on the floor, grinned with delight and hummed lightly the refrain.

The wine began to exercise its freedom and equality principles upon the heart, and all difference of rank was forgotten. Every countenance beamed with delight; every man laughed and jested, sang and drank. No one thought of the King of Prussia and his scattered army; they remembered the victory they had achieved, but the fragrant wine banished the remembrance of the conquered. *[Footnote: See Prussia; Frederick the Great.—Gebhard, p. 73.]*

Montalembert and Loudon took no part in the general mirth. They had left the table, and from an open window watched the wild and frenzied group.

"It is in vain," whispered Loudon, "we cannot influence him. The German wine lies nearer his heart than his German allies."

"But you, general, you should do what Soltikow omits or neglects. You should draw your own advantage from this tardiness of the Russian general, and pursue and crush the King of Prussia."

"I would not be here now," said Loudon, painfully, "if I could do that. My hands are bound. I dare not undertake any thing to which the allies do not agree; we can only act in concert."

A loud roar of laughter from the table silenced the two gentlemen. Soltikow had just related a merry anecdote, which made the Cossacks laugh aloud. One of the Russian generals rewarded them by throwing them two tallow-candles. This dainty little delicacy was received by them with joyful shouts.

"Let us withdraw," whispered Montalembert, "the scene becomes too Russian."

"Yes, let us go," sighed Loudon; "if we must remain here inactive, we can at least employ the time in sleep."

No one remarked the withdrawal of the two gentlemen. The gay laughter, the drinking and singing went on undisturbed, and soon became a scene of wild and drunken confusion.

"We can now also withdraw," whispered Charles Henry to Fritz Kober. "Come, come! you know we are expected."

With every possible caution, they hastened away, and only after they had left the camp of the Russians and Austrians far behind them, and passed again over the battle-field did Fritz Kober break silence. "Well," said he, sighing, "what have we to say to the king?"

"All that we have heard," said Charles Henry.

"Yes, but we have heard nothing," murmured Fritz. "I opened my ears as wide as possible, but it was all in vain. Is it not base and vile to come to Germany and speak this gibberish, not a word of which can be understood? In Germany men should be obliged to speak German, and not Russian."

"They did not speak Russian, but French," said Charles Henry; "I understood it all."

Fritz Kober stopped suddenly, and stared at his friend. "You say you understood French?"

"Yes, I was at home on the French borders. My mother was from Alsace, and there I learned French."

"You understand every thing," murmured Fritz, "but for myself, I am a poor stupid blockhead, and the king will laugh at me, for I have nothing to tell. I shall not get my commission."

"Then neither will I, Fritz; and, besides, as to what we have seen, you have as much to tell as I. You heard with your eyes and I with my ears, and the great point arrived at you know as much about as I do. The Russians and Austrians are sleeping quietly, not thinking of pursuing us. That's the principal point."

"Yes, that's true; that I can also assure the king—that will please him best. Look! Charles Henry, the day is breaking! Let us hasten on to the king. When he knows that the Austrians and Russians sleep, he will think it high time for the Prussians to be awake."

CHAPTER XV
A HERO IN MISFORTUNE

The two grenadiers returned unharmed to the village where the king had at present established his headquarters. The first rays of the morning sun were falling upon the wretched hut which was occupied by his majesty. The peaceful morning quiet was unbroken by the faintest sound, and, as if Nature had a certain reverence for the hero's slumber, even the birds were hushed, and the morning breeze blew softly against the little window, as if it would murmur a sleeping song to the king. There were no sentinels before the door; the bright morning sun alone was guarding the holy place where the unfortunate hero reposed.

Lightly, and with bated breath, the two grenadiers crept into the open hut. The utter silence disturbed them. It seemed incredible that they should find the king in this miserable place, alone and unguarded. They thought of the hordes of Cossacks which infested that region, and that a dozen of them would suffice to surround this little hut, and make prisoners of the king and his adjutants.

"I have not the courage to open the door," whispered Fritz Kober. "I fear that the king is no longer here. The Cossacks have captured him."

"God has not permitted that," said Charles Henry, solemnly; "I believe that He has guarded the king in our absence. Come, we will go to his majesty."

They opened the door and entered, and then both stood motionless, awed and arrested by what they beheld.

There, on the straw that was scantily scattered on the dirty floor, lay the king, his hat drawn partially over his face, his unsheathed sword in his hand, sleeping as quietly as if he were at his bright and beautiful Sans-Souci. "Look!" whispered Charles Henry; "thus sleeps a king, over whom God watches! But now we must awaken him."

He advanced to the king, and kneeling beside him, whispered: "Your majesty, we have returned; we bring intelligence of the Russians and Austrians."

The king arose slowly, and pushed his hat back from his brow.

"Good or bad news?" he asked.

"Good news!" said Fritz. "The Austrians and Russians have both gone to bed; they were sleepy."

"And they have no idea of pursuing your majesty," continued Charles Henry. "Loudon wished it, but Soltikow refused; he will do nothing until Daun acts."

"So you sat with them in the council of war?" asked the king, smiling.

"Yes, we were present," said Fritz Kober, with evident delight; "I saw the council, and Charles Henry heard them."

The king stood up. "You speak too loud!" he said; "you will waken these two gentlemen, who are sleeping so well. We will go outside, and you can continue your report."

He crossed the room noiselessly, and left the hut. Then seating himself before the door, on a small bench, he told the two grenadiers to give him an exact account of what they had seen and heard.

Long after they had finished speaking, the king sat silent, and apparently lost in thought. His eyes raised to heaven, he seemed to be in holy communion with the Almighty. As his eyes slowly sank, his glance fell upon the two grenadiers who stood before him, silently respectful.

"I am pleased with you, children, and this time the promise shall be kept. You shall become subordinate officers."

"In the same company?" asked Fritz Kober.

"In the same company. That is," continued the king, "if I am ever able to form companies and regiments again."

"We are not so badly off as your majesty thinks," said Fritz Kober. "Our troops have already recovered from their first terror, and as we returned we saw numbers of them entering the village. In a few hours the army can be reorganized."

"God grant that you may be right, my son!" said the king, kindly. "Go, now, into the village, and repeat the news you brought me to the soldiers. It will encourage them to hear that the enemy sleep, and do not think of pursuing us. I will prepare your commissions for you to-day. Farewell, my children!"

He bent his head slightly, and then turned to re-enter the hut and awaken his two adjutants. With a calm voice he commanded them to go into the village, and order the generals and higher officers to assemble the remnants of their regiments before the hut.

"A general march must be sounded," said the king. "The morning air will bear the sound into the distance, and when my soldiers hear it, perhaps they will return to their colors."

When the adjutants left him, the king commenced pacing slowly up and down, his hands crossed behind him.

"All is lost, all!" he murmured; "but I must wait and watch. If the stupidity or rashness of the enemy should break a mesh in the net within which I am enclosed, it is my duty to slip through with my army. Ah! how heavily this crown presses upon my head; it leaves me no moment of repose. How hard is life, and how terribly are the bright illusions of our earlier years destroyed!"

At the sound of the drum, the king shivered, and murmured to himself: "I feel now, what I never thought to feel. I am afraid my heart trembles at the thought of this encounter, as it never did in battle. The drums and trumpets call my soldiers, but they will not come. They are stretched upon the field of battle, or fleeing before the enemy. They will not come, and the sun will witness my shame and wretchedness."

The king, completely overcome, sank upon the bench, and buried his face in his hands. He sat thus for a long time. The sounds before the door became louder and louder, but the king heard them not; he still held his hands before his face. He could not see the bright array of uniforms that had assembled before the window, nor that the soldiers were swarming in from all sides. He did not hear the beating of drums, the orders to the soldiers, or military signals. Neither did he hear the door, which was gently opened by his adjutants, who had returned to inform him that his orders had been obeyed, and that the generals and staff officers were awaiting him outside the hut.

"Sire," whispered at length one of the adjutants, "your commands have been fulfilled. The generals await your majesty's pleasure."

The king allowed his hands to glide slowly from his face. "And the troops?" he asked.

"They are beginning to form."

"They are also just placing the cannon," said the second adjutant.

The king turned angrily to him. "Sir," he cried, "you lie! I have no cannon."

"Your majesty has, God be praised, more than fifty cannon," said the adjutant, firmly.

A ray of light overspread the countenance of the king, and a slight flush arose to his pale cheek. Standing up, he bowed kindly to the adjutants, and passed out among the generals, who saluted him respectfully, and pressed back to make way for their king. The king walked silently through their ranks, and then turning his head, he said:

"Gentlemen, let us see what yesterday has left us. Assemble your troops."

The generals and staff officers hurried silently away, to place themselves at the head of their regiments, and lead them before the king.

The king stood upright, his unsheathed sword in his right hand, as in the most ceremonious parade. The marching of the troops began, but it was a sad spectacle for their king. How little was left of the great and glorious army which he had led yesterday to battle! More than twenty thousand men were either killed or wounded. Thousands were flying and scattered. A few regiments had been formed with great trouble; barely five thousand men were now assembled. The king looked on with a firm eye, but his lips were tightly compressed, and his breath came heavily. Suddenly he turned to Count Dolmer, the adjutant of the Grand Duke Ferdinand of Brunswick, who had arrived a few days before with the intelligence of a victory gained at Minden. The king had invited him to remain, "I am about to overpower the Russians, remain until I can give you a like message." The king was reminded of this as he saw the count near him.

"Ah," he said, with a troubled smile, "you are waiting for the message I promised. I am distressed that I cannot make you the bearer of better news. If, however, you arrive safely at the end of your journey, and do not find Daun already in Berlin, and Contades in Magdeburg, you can assure the Grand Duke Ferdinand from me that all is not lost. Farewell, sir."

Then, bowing slightly, he advanced with a firm step to the generals. His eyes glowed and flashed once more, and his whole being reassumed its usual bold and energetic expression.

"Gentlemen," he said, in a clear voice, "fortune did not favor us yesterday, but there is no reason to despair. A day will come when we shall repay the enemy with bloody interest. I at least expect such a day; I will live for its coming, and all my thoughts and plans shall be directed toward that object. I strive for no other glory than to deliver Prussia from the conspiracy into which the whole of Europe has entered against her. I will obtain peace for my native land, but it shall be a great and honorable peace. I will accept no other: I would rather be buried under the ruins of my cannon, than accept a peace that would bring no advantages to Prussia, no fame to us

Honor is the highest, the holiest possession of individuals, as it is of nations; and Prussia, who has placed her honor in our hands, must receive it from us pure and spotless. If you agree with me, gentlemen, join me in this cry, 'Long live Prussia! Long live Prussia's honor!'"

The generals and officers joined enthusiastically in this cry, and like a mighty torrent it spread from mouth to mouth, until it reached the regiments, where it was repeated again and again. The color-bearers unfurled their tattered banners, and the shout arose from thousands of throats, "Long live Prussia's honor!"

The king's countenance was bright, but a tear seemed to glitter in his eye. He raised his glance to heaven and murmured:

"I swear to live so long as there is hope, so long as I am free! I swear only to think of death when my liberty is threatened!" Slowly his glance returned to earth, and then in a powerful voice, he cried: "Onward! onward! that has ever been Prussia's watch-word, and it shall remain so—Onward! We have a great object be fore us—we must use every effort to keep the Russians out of Berlin. The palladium of our happiness must not fall into the hands of our enemies. The Oder and the Spree must be ours—we must recover to-morrow what the enemy wrenched from us yesterday!"

"Onward! onward!" cried the army, and the words of the king bore courage and enthusiasm to all hearts.

Hope was awakened, and all were ready to follow the king; for however dark and threatening the horizon appeared, all had faith in the star of the king, and believed that it could never be extinguished.